"Close your eyes
and open your mouth..."

Jenny said, looking down into Kane's face. He lay stretched out in the grass in blissful relaxation.

Obediently he closed his eyes and opened his mouth. Jenny slowly lowered a big red strawberry onto his tongue.

"Now, you have to admit," she said, "this is the juiciest, sweetest strawberry you have ever tasted in your entire life."

"Not a doubt about it." She offered him another strawberry, which he caught between his pursed lips. Eyes still closed, he slowly ate the berry. "Not as sweet as you, though," he murmured....

Dear Reader,

Welcome to Silhouette—experience the magic of the wonderful world where two people fall in love. Meet heroines that will make you cheer for their happiness, and heroes (be they the boy next door or a handsome, mysterious stranger) who will win your heart. Silhouette Romance reflects the magic of love—sweeping you away with books that will make you laugh and cry, heartwarming, poignant stories that will move you time and time again.

In the coming months we're publishing romances by many of your all-time favorites, such as Diana Palmer, Brittany Young, Sondra Stanford and Annette Broadrick. Your response to these authors and our other Silhouette Romance authors has served as a touchstone for us, and we're pleased to bring you more books with Silhouette's distinctive medley of charm, wit and—above all—*romance*.

I hope you enjoy this book and the many stories to come. Experience the magic!

Sincerely,

Tara Hughes
Senior Editor
Silhouette Books

MONA VAN WIEREN

Rhapsody in Bloom

Silhouette **Romance**

Published by Silhouette Books New York

America's Publisher of Contemporary Romance

To my mother,
who let me get on that plane to Africa

SILHOUETTE BOOKS
300 E. 42nd St., New York, N.Y. 10017

Copyright © 1989 by Mona van Wieren

ISBN: 0-373-08630-X

First Silhouette Books printing February 1989

Printed in the U.S.A.

MONA VAN WIEREN

was born in Holland where she started writing short stories in Dutch. She met her American husband in Amsterdam and later married him in Kenya, where he was a Peace Corps volunteer. Her husband's work as a development economist has also given them the opportunity to spend several years in Ghana and Indonesia.

"Writing in English was a challenge at first, but with the encouragement of my husband I kept going and finally made it into print."

Mona now lives in Virginia with her husband and three children.

She has also published books under the pseudonym Karen van der Zee.

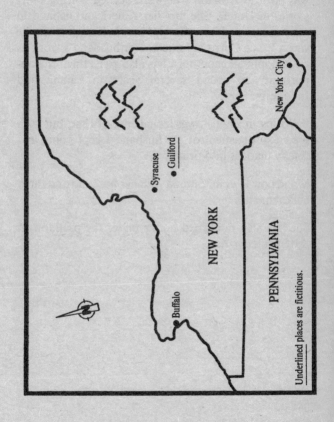

Underlined places are fictitious.

Chapter One

Jennifer McCarthy?"

Jenny gave a start and almost lost her balance when she heard the deep, male voice so close to her. Lost in thought, she had not noticed anyone approach. Sitting on her haunches, looking up at the giant towering over her, she felt distinctly at a disadvantage. This was no ordinary male of the Guilford variety. This one had stepped straight out of somebody's fantasy. Maybe even her own.

Hastily she came to her feet, dropping the trowel. Wiping her muddy hands on her jeans, she smiled at the stranger. He looked rather out of place here in his tailored suit and shiny black shoes. This muddy patch of land had never seen shoes like his.

"Sorry, didn't mean to startle you," he said, dark eyes looking amused. "My name is Kane Powell. Are you Jennifer McCarthy?"

Jennifer. Nobody had ever called her Jennifer. It sounded strange. She nodded, hiding her hands behind her back. "Yes, yes. I didn't hear you coming." He was very good-looking, tall and well-built, with thick dark hair, brown eyes and a very impressive Grecian nose—impressive partly because it was rather too big for perfection. Anyway, who wanted perfection? Perfection was boring.

The man was smiling at her, radiating charm and sophistication. Jenny felt a stirring of interest. She liked tall men, she liked brown eyes. Maybe because they were everything she was not. She was short, blond and blue-eyed. As a teenager she had dreamed of being tall, dark and sultry, of looking more mature and sophisticated. Her teenage years had been riddled with insecurities. Once in college, she had discovered that it was quite all right to be small, blond and blue-eyed.

The man looked at the trowel, then back at her, giving her a curious glance. "What were you doing?"

"Digging for worms."

"Going fishing?"

She laughed. "Not today. I was just checking. I'll plant my vegetable garden here."

"And worms are bad?"

"Worms are good. They aerate the soil." Not a gardener, this one, she thought. Not that he looked like one, either. She wondered what such a man was doing here in her little, small-town nursery. He looked like he'd just walked out of New York City—Wall Street, Madison Avenue, something like that. On the other hand, his cultured tones pointed further north, Boston perhaps. Or maybe he was a British count disguised as an American. Maybe he even owned a castle or a country estate.

Dream on, she told herself derisively.

She smiled at him politely. "May I help you?"

"I'm not sure." There were laughing lights in his eyes and his gaze was focused not on her face but higher up, on her head. She wondered what was so interesting about her hair. Then suddenly he leaned forward, hand reaching out to her. "Allow me...there's something in your hair." Before she could react, he carefully picked up something with his fingers, put it on the back of his hand and showed it to her.

It was a tiny caterpillar, colorful, hairy, creeping along now on the big brown hand.

Jenny laughed. "I've got things crawling on me all the time." *What a thing to say!* she thought, hearing her own words. "Occupational hazard," she added quickly.

"I don't doubt it." He examined the creeping thing on his hand. "It's beautiful," he commented. "Look at the colors. A piece of art."

"Yes." She smiled with delight, meeting his eyes in a flash of some deeper understanding, some recognition of part of herself—almost embarrassing. Quickly she lowered her gaze.

For a moment they watched the caterpillar as it inched its way up the sleeve of his light gray suit. Then he went down on his haunches and gently put it in the grass. "There you go, buddy. Go find your friends." Straightening again, he suddenly frowned. "Oh...should I have exterminated the poor creature? Will he damage your plants?"

Jenny shook her head. "No, not this one. All he'll do is change into a pretty butterfly."

"You like butterflies?"

She nodded. "Works of art."

His smile warmed her. She liked his face, the way the strong, angular features softened when he smiled. She liked the way he had put the caterpillar back in the grass, gently so as not to hurt it. She looked into the laughing brown eyes, then glanced away. *Don't be a fool,* she told herself. *He's a fantasy man. He wouldn't stand up to the wear and tear of daily life.*

Wouldn't it be nice, though, just for a change. The only single male she knew in Guilford was Billy James who ran the hardware store—friendly enough, but utterly boring. Billy's conversations were limited to the newest kind of paint and last week's football game. Now and then he would ask her out, invitations she always declined. He loved his beer too much, and drove his Bronco too fast.

Suddenly she felt the outrageous desire to be swept off her feet by someone like this dark-eyed stranger, a man from a different world. Visions of candlelight dinners and trips to exotic places flashed through her mind. There you go again, she thought drily. For all you know he's a bookkeeper with a penchant for expensive clothes.

"Do you plant a big garden?" he asked, looking around.

She sighed, letting her eyes sweep over the land. At the far end of her property were the trees: dogwoods that had finished blooming now, pines and maples. The grass was green again, the sky blue. In front of the house a vibrant profusion of tulips and azaleas bloomed in a multitude of dancing colors.

"I plant all this," she answered, pointing out the cleared area. "It's not all for myself, though. I sell most of it." Every summer she would have her stand in front of the nursery and Old Jim would mind it most days. He was seventy years old and loved sitting by the road and talking to the customers, telling them Jenny grew the sweetest strawberries and the biggest tomatoes in all of New York State.

"It's so peaceful here." He ran a large brown hand through the thick mane of his hair and smiled. "Quiet, peaceful."

"Some call it boring, stagnant."

He raised his brows. "Do you?"

"Actually, no. I love the outdoors. I love living here, seeing things grow and bloom, the change of the seasons. Only..." She shrugged, looking away.

"Only what?"

Only I wish there were people I could feel some inner connection with. There's something missing in my life. The words were only thoughts. You didn't say these things to strangers. "Only I wouldn't mind a little excitement now and then," she said instead. "Not much goes on in a small town like this." *Oh, Lord,* she thought, *I hope he doesn't take that as a come on.*

He nodded. "Yes, I suppose if you live here all year around it would feel that way." He gestured at the greenhouse. "What's in there?"

"Mostly seedlings at the moment. I start all my plants from seed early in the year. Then I transplant what I need for my own garden and sell the rest. A lot of people have gardens around here. Would you like to see it?"

"Thank you, yes."

She walked ahead of him, conscious of her dirty jeans and sneakers. Well, that's the way it was. She wondered why he had come to see her. Here she was yakking away about her business instead of figuring out what he wanted.

Maybe he was lost and needed directions. Maybe his car was broken down and he wanted to use the phone. Maybe for the first time in history, the Peacock Inn was full and he had no place to go. She could invite him to stay here. She'd share her split pea soup with him and he could sleep on the lumpy old couch. After that he wouldn't want to leave. He'd fall in love with her, take her away on cruises and trips and marry her and they'd live happily ever after.

She sighed inwardly. Ah, this was the stuff fantasies were made of. Well, some fantasies, anyway. The problem with her job was that she had too much time to think and to daydream. Often there was no one to talk to. And talking to plants and flowers was singularly unsatisfying since they didn't talk back.

She gave him a quick, sideways glance. Besides, he was all wrong. She knew his type. The circles her parents moved in were rife with men of his sort—successful, influential, power hungry. At least, he certainly looked like one of them, despite his charm. She'd rejected her parents' lifestyle and the kind of men they wanted for her years ago. So what was she thinking of? I must be crazy, she thought.

They passed a long row of blackberry bushes. Her grandfather had planted those years ago. He had also planted the apple and pear trees in the back of the house. What she couldn't eat herself, she sold.

It was warm and humid in the greenhouse and the air smelled of moist earth and green, growing things. She liked the smell, had been familiar with it since she was a child and visited her grandfather here. Long tables ran the length of the small enclosure, laden with trays of delicate green plants. She would never tire of seeing seedlings grow, never cease to be amazed at the miracle of life, the beauty springing from tiny seeds.

"This side is vegetables and herbs," she explained, wondering if he really cared or was just being polite. "The other side is flowers—marigolds, petunias, impatiens, that sort of thing. I sell a lot of flowers in the spring when people are ready to have some color in their yards. Do you have a yard?"

He grinned. "I'm not sure. As it stands now, I have about three acres of out-of-control jungle. I've no idea what's lurking beneath the wilderness."

She felt a rush of excitement. Three acres of out-of-control jungle! She knew where that was! "The Cleever house?" she asked almost breathlessly. "You bought the Cleever house?"

He laughed, apparently amused by her enthusiasm. "I did. Do you approve?"

"We've all been wondering what would happen to the place. It's been empty so long, you see, and that isn't good for a house. And the grounds, the garden . . . well you know about that. It's a crime the way the place looks. It could be so beautiful."

He nodded. "And it will be again. The house needs a lot of work and the grounds need to be overhauled completely. I need a professional. That's why I'm here. I wonder if you could give me the names of some reputable landscape companies. I suppose there are some in Syracuse?"

She felt a sinking feeling of disappointment. It had been a secret dream to tame the wilderness around the Cleever house herself, make it beautiful, a piece of art. On more than one occasion she had walked longingly around the grounds, thinking of the possibilities.

She looked straight at him. "I can do it," she said, her heart hammering. "I've done a number of gardens here in Guilford." *But all small. None of them anything like the Clever place.* But she could do it, she knew it. It would be the challenge of her life, but she felt equal to it.

Surprise flashed in the brown eyes. "You're a landscape designer?"

"No, I'm not. I just like doing it."

She saw him frown and suddenly she felt like a child with her dirty jeans and muddy hands, her hair in a ponytail, no makeup—a child who liked to play in the mud. He doesn't believe I'm capable, she thought, looking at his doubting face. All he sees is this little greenhouse run by a skinny blonde with no real qualifications. Well, she couldn't blame him, could she? She was not a trained landscape architect.

Most people around Guilford would never dream of engaging one. It was nothing more than a country town, too far from New York City to be a commuter community. But I'm good, she thought. Damn good.

He raised his eyebrows. "You just like doing it?"

"Landscaping. Designing people's gardens. And I'm good at it," she added boldly. It was what she loved more than anything else: taking a raw piece of land around a new house and creating a garden out of it, or redesigning neglected gardens around older houses. All her creative juices would start to flow and she could indulge her imagination. She loved the unusual, the unexpected. Ideas blossomed in her mind as she searched for a different approach, something original, a unique design.

He was shaking his head. "I'm sure this is a job that needs all the resources of a fully equipped landscaping company, which isn't saying anything about your capabilities. Looking around, I can see you have more than one green thumb."

Disappointment was bitter in her mouth. It would be wonderful to do a garden again. Apart from that, she had to admit, she needed the money. Well, she wasn't going to tell him that. She had her pride, if not much more. She pasted on a smile. "If you're quite sure. I do have a fair amount of experience, but if you'd feel more comfortable with a qualified landscape architect, there are some very good ones in Syracuse. There's Greenscape Inc. and Melton's Landscape and Grounds. The numbers are in the book." Her voice was calm, her smile still in place. She felt very noble, very mature. But deep down, angry feelings smoldered.

"Thank you." He examined his watch and frowned. "I have to get back to the city. Thank you very much for showing me around, Ms. McCarthy."

Ms. McCarthy. It didn't happen often that someone called her Ms. She smiled stiffly. "You're welcome." She opened the door of the greenhouse and they went outside into the watery spring sunshine. She watched him as he slid his lean body into the shiny gray Continental and drove away.

There was nothing wrong with his car. He was not lost. He did have a place to go to. He didn't need her or her couch or her split pea soup. So much for that fantasy. And so much for her dream of landscaping the Cleever grounds. He didn't need her to do that, either.

Sighing, she wiped a muddy hand across her forehead. She felt hopelessly deflated. Mr. Kane Powell was obviously a high-powered man. He exuded self-confidence and sophistication. He'd be used to dealing with competent and influential professionals, people with credentials and expertise. No wonder he wasn't going to suffer an amateur like her. Oh, damn him, she thought unreasonably.

Slowly she walked into the house to make herself a cup of coffee. The sink was stacked full of dirty dishes from yesterday's dinner and this morning's breakfast. She'd forgotten all about lunch, she just realized. She shrugged. She wasn't hungry. Making a face, she turned away from the dishes. She didn't feel like doing them now. There was work to do outside, work more important and interesting than housework. Her coffee made, she took the mug outside with her.

Kane Powell was on her mind as she worked, staking out rows for the various vegetables to be planted. Mr. High and Mighty. Who did he think he was anyway, to reject her offer to do the job? He hadn't even wanted to discuss it! What did he know about her and her work? Nothing! Zilch! And she didn't know much more about him, either, apart from his name, the fact that he had bought the Cleever house and that he looked rather well-off.

No, there was something else.

She thought of the tiny caterpillar crawling on the sleeve of his impeccable suit, and of the gentleness with which he had deposited the little creature back into the grass.

Kane Powell found himself smiling as he drove down the thruway toward New York, thinking about Jennifer. Not much to her—short, slim and softly pretty. Something about her had touched him. Was it her mouth, wide, generous, smiling? Or the blue, blue eyes that were not at all childish or innocent but hid thoughts and experiences he could only guess at? Maybe it was her voice. He could hear it again in his mind, the soft singsong tone of it. Sexy, definitely sexy. He grinned again.

Buying the house might be the biggest mistake of his life. How often would he really be there to enjoy it? The past few years he'd been out of the country more than in. But it would have to stop, this mad racing around the world. What he had been searching for was not any place out there. It was something inside himself. Maybe the house in its quiet setting would help calm him down.

He glanced at his watch again and frowned. He shouldn't have stayed as long as he had. He had a lot of work to do. Files to read and portfolios to look through. And he had to call Tokyo and see if he could get Yokomasi to get his butt over here and be present at the exhibition of his paintings. He wouldn't make it back in time to call those landscaping companies in Syracuse and see when they could come and have a look at the grounds. It would have to wait till tomorrow.

It was just after six when he put the key in the door and entered his apartment. It was cool and quiet and clean inside. There were flowers on the coffee table. Mrs. DeRosa did more than clean. Sometimes she would leave a batch of fresh cookies or a cutting from a paper or magazine. Still, the place had never felt like home. It never could be. It was too empty and too quiet and too neat. He crossed the living room and entered his home office. He had worked for about fifteen minutes when the doorbell rang.

He pushed the button of the intercom. "Yes?"

"Kane? It's me, Vicky."

"Vicky!"

"Are you going to open the door or do I have to scale the building and climb in through the window?"

He laughed as he buzzed the door open.

When she was there, moments later, she flew into his arms. He held her tight for a moment until she wriggled loose.

"How have you been?" she inquired, tilting her head a little and scrutinizing him closely. "That tan is sinful, you know," she added enviously.

He grinned, looking at her with appreciation. Her auburn hair danced in short, loose curls around her head. Her skin was fair, her eyes large and clear gray. She was beautiful, Vicky, but a real tan she would never acquire. "I'm fine. And you?"

"Busy, busy. My students drive me crazy and finals kill me."

"I'm honored you could spare me some time," he said lightly, surprised to see the sudden sadness in her eyes.

"I wanted to be with you tonight."

He smiled, wondering about the strange expression on Vicky's face. She swallowed visibly.

"I thought you might like some company. We can go out, have something to eat." Her smile was forced. "You could take me to one of those indecently expensive places full of celebrities." She searched his face. "You're all right?"

He frowned. "I'm fine, Vicky. Is something wrong?"

"I thought..." She smiled, brightly, too brightly. "Never mind."

He took her shoulders. "No, tell me. What is it?"

She hesitated, obviously wrestling with something. "It's the twenty-seventh today," she whispered.

He closed his eyes. "I'd forgotten," he said, feeling a curious mixture of pain and guilt.

Jenny was standing at the counter making herself a peanut butter sandwich and thinking of the Cleever house grounds and about Kane Powell. She couldn't get him out of her mind, and the disappointment hadn't faded.

She looked up when she heard a car stop in front of the house. It was her mother's dark green Mercedes. She emerged from the car and quickly walked up to the kitchen door, amazingly steady on her high heels. Bracing herself mentally, Jenny smiled at her mother as she came inside.

"Hi, Mom. I was just having some lunch. Sit down. Can I get you a sandwich?"

"No thanks. I'm having lunch with Carol later. We're planning the benefit dinner."

"A cup of coffee?"

"Instant?"

Jenny smiled indulgently. "Of course, Mom. When was the last time you had a real cup of coffee at my place? And let me tell you a secret: once you're used to instant you won't even like the real stuff anymore."

"I'll pass, thanks. I drink too much coffee as it is."

Jenny poured herself a glass of milk and sat down at the table, taking a big bite from her sandwich and examining her mother. She'd been to the beauty parlor, Jenny noticed. Every hair in place. Flawless makeup. Discreet perfume. Elegant shirtdress. Jenny tucked a strand of hair behind her ear and swallowed her food, aware of her mother's scrutiny.

"Jenny, why don't you do something about your hair? Have it cut. One of those short cuts would flatter your face."

"I like it this way. Besides, they say men like long hair."

"Men?"

"Yeah, you know, the males of the species. Or had you given up on me already?"

Her mother frowned. "I hadn't thought about that."

"Sure you have. You keep hoping some nice, intelligent, educated man with a large bank account will come by and rescue me from my folly, make a respectable woman out of me—with clean fingernails and nice clothes."

"Oh, Jenny, you're exaggerating."

Jenny smiled sweetly. "No, I'm not." She took another bite of her sandwich. Through her lashes she watched her mother who was frowning and tapping her long nails on the table.

"I came by to ask you to come for Sunday dinner. Suzanne is coming and she's bringing David."

"All the more reason for me to stay away," Jenny said lightly. Her perfect sister Suzanne with her perfect man were perfect bores.

"You don't like David very much, do you?"

"No, Mom, I don't."

"He does very well for himself."

"So he never fails to tell us. He's a pompous, arrogant jerk."

"Jenny!"

She laughed out loud. "Oh, Mom, don't look like that! And I don't think Dad likes him very much either." She shrugged. "Anyway, I'll be there. Can I bring anything?" It was a question asked out of politeness. She already knew the answer. Her mother didn't trust her vegetarian concoctions. *Jenny, you need to eat meat sometimes,* she'd say. *No, I don't,* Jenny would answer. *Rice and beans is perfectly good food.*

She'd had endless, futile arguments with her mother about her eating habits. Her mother knew best. She'd always known best and wasn't about to try any of the vegetarian dishes Jenny cooked.

"I found a wonderful recipe, bulgur wheat, lentils..."

"No, thanks. I've got it all planned." She stood up restlessly and glanced at her watch. Then she stared down at the dishes in the sink and frowned.

"Sweetheart, why don't you at least rinse them? You're going to need a steel brush to get that egg off the plate now that it's been sitting there all morning."

Jenny leaned back in her chair. "I have one just for that purpose. And you know something, Mom? I'm twenty-six years old and if I don't want to rinse my dishes, I don't have to."

"But it makes washing them so much easier! It saves you work! Not to speak of the sanitary aspect of it." She surveyed the kitchen with ill-concealed disapproval. "And that garbage can... you ought to empty it more often, sweetheart."

Jenny put the remnants of her sandwich down on the plate and came to her feet. She put her hands on her mother's shoulders and looked solemnly into her eyes. "I promise you that at the first sign of a rat or cockroach I'll call the exterminators."

"Oh, Jenny, why can't you be serious?"

"I am serious. I don't like rats."

Her mother let out a long-suffering sigh and shook her head in despair.

Jenny moved away and sat down again, draining the last of her milk. "You may as well accept it, Mom. I'm a hopeless case."

"I never said that."

"But you're thinking it. I know I'm not living up to your expectations. I'm a worthless nobody, a college dropout, a menial worker with muddy hands, broken nails, a messy kitchen and dirty dishes." She gave a theatrical sigh. "All your good intentions, all the money you spent on me, all your efforts...pffsht, down the drain."

"Oh, Jenny, there you go again."

"Nothing will ever become of me," she went on, warming to the subject. "No self-respecting man will ever want me. I'll be growing radishes for the rest of my life. I won't produce any grandchildren for you. I'll die of malnutrition surrounded by dirty dishes and rats feeding from the overflowing garbage can." She sighed and gave her mother a despairing look. "It's all so tragic it makes me cry. But at least you have Suzanne. Suzanne will make up for me, I'm sure."

Her mother looked pained. "You're always making a joke out of everything. I wish I knew how to talk some sense into you."

Jenny shook her head decisively. "Give up, Mom. You might as well face the bitter truth: your younger daughter is a lost cause."

"Well, she certainly is today." She picked up her handbag from the chair and moved to the door. "I'm on my way. I'll see you Sunday, then?"

"I'll be there. Maybe I'll bring some Indian carrot pudding for dessert. Very nutritious. I'm sure you'll like it." She wasn't sure why she was goading her mother. She just couldn't resist.

"Don't bother. We'll have a lemon soufflé."

She watched her mother drive away, then turned and kicked a chair. "Damn," she muttered to herself.

After work the next day, Jenny decided on impulse to go to the Cleever house grounds. As she tramped dispiritedly through the overgrown greenery, she had the sudden eerie feeling she was being followed.

She stood still, listening, her stomach cramping with fear. Twigs snapped and leaves rustled not too far behind her. Someone else was in the garden.

Why had she come here, anyway? It had been a stupid idea. It was getting dark already. But she'd wanted to come here just one more time, to walk through this wilderness and say goodbye to a dream. One more time to visualize what it would be like if she had a free hand to do as she pleased, to transform this jungle into a garden again.

But she wasn't going to stand there and wait for whoever was back there. Heart thudding, legs trembling, she moved forward, arms stretched out to keep branches and twigs from scraping her face. Weeds and undergrowth had spread rampantly in the last few years and it was hard to see where the paths were. But she'd been here enough times to know how to find her way back to the house.

She'd never known such fear. Her clothes were damp with perspiration. What if it were some maniac who'd attack her? Nobody would hear or notice a thing here. Maybe this was the chance she'd get to practice her self-defense techniques. Good God, she hoped she could remember them. It had been years since she'd taken the course. As she struggled on through the greenery, stumbling, running, she frantically began to search her memory. Her breathing was ragged and painful and she tried with all her might to stay calm and keep her wits about her.

She ran as quickly as her legs would carry her, aware that behind her the footsteps were coming faster, too. Branches creaked and twigs snapped ominously behind her and her blood throbbed in her head as she blindly plodded forward, too afraid now to even look where she placed her feet. Once she nearly tripped on a stone, but she kept herself going, arms flailing, her lungs pumping for air. A thorny twig scratched her face and she felt the stinging pain across her cheek.

Panic engulfed her when suddenly she found herself tripping, falling headlong in the muddy, leafy muck. She scrambled up as fast as she could, but it was too late. Before she'd managed to come to her feet, a man broke through the brush. She saw a flash of blue denim, a leather jacket and a flat sports cap.

He raced toward her at an alarming speed. With desperate strength she pushed her feet to the ground and lurched forward, away from him.

Chapter Two

"Wait!" he called.

She wasn't about to. In a panic she ran off, but he grabbed her arm before she'd moved more than a few yards.

She stopped, wincing at the pain in her arm and stared at him. He released her arm.

"Good God," he muttered. "It's you."

It was the nose she recognized. Kane Powell. And then fury rushed like fire through her, replacing the panic. "How dare you!" she choked, tears of rage blinding her eyes. "How dare you do this to me!"

"Do what to you?"

"Don't play dumb!" she cried, gasping for breath. "How dare you chase me like that!" Her legs were shaking with anger and exhaustion both and the pounding of her heart was drumming in her ears.

One dark eyebrow rose sardonically. "How dare I chase you? This is my property. You were trespassing."

Trespassing? It had never occurred to her to think that she was trespassing. Over the years she'd come here many times, looking, dreaming. In some ways, this place was hers. Trespassing, he said. Well, true as that was technically, he had no right to scare the living daylights out of her.

She struggled for breath. "You scared me senseless! Didn't you know that? I had visions of being...oh, never mind." She wiped her forehead, which was wet with perspiration.

"Raped and murdered?" he supplied. "I was merely checking to see what you were doing here. Only I didn't know it was you. I didn't recognize you with that scarf on your hair. But I'm sorry I frightened you."

She'd put the scarf on to keep the branches and twigs from tearing at her hair. She hadn't recognized him immediately either in casual clothes. He didn't look at all like the man she'd met a few days ago. The sleek polish was gone. Yet despite the change in clothes, his male appeal was still there and had acquired an interesting edge of ruggedness. Now that her fear had eased, she was suddenly quite conscious of his vibrant maleness.

Jenny turned away abruptly, her anger not yet appeased. She tore off the scarf and stuffed it into her pocket. Her hands were wet from the ground and she wiped them on her jeans as she walked on.

"What were you doing here?" he asked, following her.

"Nothing."

"Not very smart to come here when it's about to get dark."

She swung around. "Oh, for God's sake, stop it! I know that! But I couldn't come until after working hours!"

"Why did you come?"

"I've come here lots of times. I like it here." She walked on doggedly. He could ask all he wanted, she wasn't about to tell him the real reason.

"To commune with nature?"

"Yes." Why not? It was as good a reason as any. The house appeared in front of her, empty and forlorn in the semidarkness. Soon it would no longer be empty. Soon people would live here and the garden would be restored and she could never come here again.

"Can I give you a ride home?" he asked.

"No, thanks," she said coolly. "My pickup is parked by the road."

He frowned. "The gate was locked. How did you get in?"

"Through a hole in the fence."

His laugh was low and amused. "Through a hole in the fence," he repeated. "Not very ladylike, is it?"

She gave an exasperated sigh and spread out her arms. "Have a look. Do I look like a lady?"

His grin widened as he slowly, deliberately, let his gaze travel over her, from the top of her head to her toes, lingering on her more obvious female attributes.

She glared at him angrily, knowing she had invited his appraisal, knowing too that she looked a mess with her clothes muddy from her fall and with leaves and twigs sticking to her.

He shook his head. "Not a lady, no. A woman, yes. Definitely a woman."

"Oh, shut up!" She felt heat rise to her face.

"A little tomboy, then?" His hand reached out and touched her cheek with surprising gentleness. "You have a scratch there."

"I certainly do," she twisted her face away from his touch. "Thanks to you." She turned around once more to stalk down the drive toward the gate. She assumed it wasn't locked now. She wasn't about to crawl through a hole in the fence with him watching.

He followed her out the gate and watched as she climbed into the pickup, shutting the door for her.

"Come again," he invited. "But do let me know you're here, for safety's sake."

"I won't bother you again, don't worry."

"You didn't bother me. Actually, you made my evening." There was mild mockery in his voice.

She didn't answer him, just turned the key in the ignition and drove off.

Early the next morning, Saturday, she was on her knees transplanting tomato seedlings when she heard Kane Powell's cheerful "good morning" as he came toward her along the path. Her pulse quickened at the sight of him. He was dressed in faded jeans, a blue and white plaid work shirt, sneakers, and the leather cap he'd worn the night before. The sleeves of his shirt were rolled up, exposing deeply bronzed arms, which he crossed now as he looked down at her with a grin.

"The worm count was high enough, I presume?"

She nodded silently, carefully pushing up soil around one of the fragile seedlings.

"What are these?" he asked.

She looked up. "What? These? Beefsteaks."

"Beefsteaks? You could have fooled me. What are beefsteaks?"

She gave him an incredulous look. "Tomatoes, of course. Don't you know a tomato plant when you see one?"

He shook his head. "Sorry, no. I never paid much attention."

Jenny made no comment and went on putting the little plants in the ground. He went down on his haunches and watched her silently for several minutes.

"How about lunch?" he asked after a while.

She shook her head. "No thanks, I need to finish these." She didn't want to go out to lunch with him. She didn't want to hear about his wretched house and his wretched garden. After the previous night she wanted nothing more to do with him or his garden.

"How about if I give you a hand with these?"

She stared at him in surprise, and he laughed. "I've been watching you. I think I can manage."

"You'll get dirty."

"So I will. I'm sure it will wash off again. And when we're finished I'll take you out to lunch."

She took a deep breath. "It's very nice of you, but I can't take the time. There are more plants in the greenhouse. I'd like to do them today." She kept her gaze lowered, at the ground, at her busy hands.

"I had hoped you might take pity on me, a stranger in a new town. You're the only person I know."

"My heart bleeds for you."

"Did I say something wrong?"

"Not a thing."

"Are you still mad at me for frightening you last night?"

"Yes," she said bluntly. "And I have no time for lunch, or for chitchat."

"I thought you were a nice person. I rather liked you when I met you a couple of days ago. Why all the acid suddenly?"

"It must be the tomatoes."

"Tomatoes are sweet."

She sighed. "Oh, never mind." She pushed the empty flat away and pulled another one toward her.

He reached over and lifted out one of the seedlings. "All right, let's see if we can make this a cooperative effort." He lowered the small plant into the depression Jenny had made. She watched his hands, strong, brown hands, moving the fragile plants with gentle care. No rings adorned his fingers, she noted, not that it meant anything.

He took another plant from the flat. Well, she thought, if this is what he wants who am I to object? Mr. Rich on his knees in the mud—who'd ever believe it? "Well, Mr. Powell, I can see there is no stopping you—is there?"

"Please call me Kane. May I call you Jennifer?"

"Everybody calls me Jenny."

"Jenny is a little girl's name," he stated, carefully pushing the soil up around the plant's stem. "And if everybody calls you Jenny, I'd like to call you Jennifer."

Jenny said nothing. She did not like him deciding what to call her. She found it presumptuous, to say the least.

"Do you mind?"

"Yes. It doesn't sound like me."

"It is your name, isn't it?"

"Yes. But it's not what I'm called."

"Jennifer is a good name. It has substance, character. I like it. Jenny is . . . it's sweet, childish, undefined. You're a woman. Why not have a woman's name?"

She eyed him warily. Was he making fun of her? She was determined not to show her irritation. "My name is Jenny," she said coolly. "If that isn't good enough for you, by all means call me Ms. McCarthy."

He threw back his head and gave a bellow of a laugh. "I like that, I really like that."

It was hard not to smile, but she managed, just barely. "I'm glad you're amused."

"And you, obviously, are not. What's the matter, Ms. McCarthy? Pray tell, I'm intrigued."

She didn't answer. Instead, she came to her feet and went to the greenhouse for more plants. Yes, what was the matter with her? Certainly something was. She was attracted to him, she couldn't possibly deny it. Yet he irritated her; he made her feel off balance.

When she returned he was lying on his back in the grass, looking up at the clouds, hands behind his head. For some reason it disturbed her to see him stretched out so lazily on her grass and she wondered briefly about the lean, muscular body under the covering of clothes. She quickly dispelled the image.

"Look up, Ms. McCarthy, there's an elephant in the sky."

She groaned. "Oh please, stop it. I give up. You win." She plonked the tray of plants on the ground. "What's wrong with Jenny, for Pete's sake?"

In one smooth, fluid movement he sat up, his face close to hers. "I told you. It sounds childish. It doesn't fit." His eyes looked into hers, and again she felt a slight tightening of her stomach muscles.

She withdrew slightly. "You don't know a thing about me. How do you know what fits me?"

He put his hand over his heart in a theatrical gesture and grinned. "Instinct."

She looked up at the sky and rolled her eyes. "Call me whatever you want."

"Thank you, Jennifer." He flashed her an irresistible smile, which she ignored. She refused to be taken in by his charm. No doubt it was only a surface thing. Underneath he was sharp and ruthless and calculating as any New York businessman. He didn't fool her for a minute.

Yet she found it impossible to decline his offer for lunch when he made it again an hour later. Her irritation had somehow dissipated. After all, he was helping her and he was being disgustingly charming and she was a sucker for warm brown eyes.

"I'm starving," he said, as they walked up to the house to clean up. "I didn't have any breakfast."

"Why not? Are you one of those people who lives on coffee?"

He grinned. "No, but I had no way to cook myself anything. They've been redoing all the wiring in the house and there's no electricity."

"You moved in already? I thought—"

"I slept in a sleeping bag on the floor. I won't be moving in properly until the fall."

They entered the kitchen and Jenny emptied the sink of dirty dishes and found him a clean towel. "I'll change and clean up in the bathroom. I won't be long."

She scrubbed her hands, but her nails wouldn't come clean. She hated wearing gloves, preferring the feel of good, rich soil on her hands as she worked. A streak of mud decorated her left cheek. Grimacing at herself, she wiped it off. She took the rubber band out of her hair and shook it loose. It fell in a smooth, shiny curtain below her shoulders. In the bedroom she found a clean pair of jeans and a striped blouse and quickly put them on. Now a little makeup. She never used much and normally didn't bother with any while she worked. A few minutes later she was back in the kitchen.

Kane surveyed her for a silent moment and she felt uneasy under his regard.

"Do I have another bug in my hair?"

He laughed. "No. But you have beautiful hair."

"Thank you. And please tell that to my mother. She keeps nagging me to cut it off and get one of those short, fashionable hairstyles."

"You live with your mother?"

She stared at him. "Here?" She began to laugh. "My mother is afraid to visit me. Afraid she'll catch something. No she lives with my father in her own beautiful clean house outside Syracuse."

"You think they'll let me into a restaurant like this?" Kane looked down at his jeans, the knees wet and muddy.

"This is Guilford. At Sammy's Superduper Diner nobody cares what you look like."

"Sammy's Superduper Diner? That's a real place?"

"Absolutely genuine."

She followed him out to the car and he opened the passenger door and helped her in. Not bad, she thought, as she leaned back on the luxurious seat. Quite a difference from her own beat-up red pickup truck. It had been her grandfather's and was ancient, but it was perfect for her work and she enjoyed driving it.

He slid behind the wheel and started the engine. She watched his brown hands on the steering wheel. He had quite a tan for this early in the year.

"Do you live in New York City?" she asked.

"I do. I have an apartment."

"You have a sunlamp?"

He gave her a startled look. "A what?"

"A sunlamp. For when you want a suntan in the winter." She tried to keep her face straight, but she could feel the laughter bubble in her throat. "You look beautifully tanned. I thought maybe you spend fifteen minutes every day under a sunlamp."

He threw his head back and laughed. "My God, where did you get a notion like that?"

She tapped her head. "It just popped up. It happens now and then."

Over a grilled cheese sandwich in Sammy's Superduper Diner, Jenny discovered that Kane was an importer of foreign art, a fact that quite impressed her but which she was determined not to show.

"So," she said, "how do you find all those masterpieces to import?"

"I travel a lot." His voice was dry.

"Sounds like fun."

He rolled his eyes. "A laugh a minute."

She narrowed her eyes. "Don't sound so blasé."

He shrugged. "I am blasé. Not to speak of jaded and world-weary and plane and hotel weary."

"Such a hard life," she nodded pseudosympathetically. "Tell me all about it."

"I don't want to distress you," he mocked.

She picked up her napkin. "Don't worry, I've got my hankie ready."

For years now he had traveled to the most exotic places finding artworks of all sorts—paintings and sculptures and rugs and brass and pottery, he explained. He looked for artists with bona fide talent, and his findings were of the more exclusive kind. The art was sold by the poshest of art dealers and galleries in New York, Boston and San Francisco to the discriminating wealthy of America.

Jenny was fascinated by his stories. She forgot to eat the second half of her sandwich. She forgot she was in Sammy's Superduper Diner. All she was aware of was Kane Powell and his somewhat bizarre tales of the faraway places he visited and the colorful characters with whom he conducted his business. He'd just returned from a trip to Polynesia, where—on a tiny island—he had discovered a withered old woman painter creating the most wildly imaginative oil paintings, bordering on the erotic.

"She must be over a hundred years old. She's about four and a half feet tall and weighs less then eighty pounds, I'm sure. But her eyes! Sharp as black diamonds! Not a tooth in her mouth and practically bald, but can she paint!"

She liked his enthusiasm, the way he talked about people and places rather than money. "Where does this grandmama get her ideas?"

He laughed. "I've been wondering the same thing."

A gum-chewing waitress filled their coffee cups for the second time, smiling coyly at Kane. "Can I get you anything else?"

"Not for me. Jennifer?"

"No thanks. Just coffee."

"I've done too much talking," Kane stated. "Tell me something about yourself. How did you come to start a nursery?"

"It was my grandfather's. He started it to keep busy after he retired. It wasn't meant as a serious, profitmaking business. He'd always enjoyed gardening as a hobby, you see. He grew vegetables and flowers in the greenhouse early in the year and when planting time came around he'd sell the small plants to gardeners in the area. It was a good way to stay busy and to meet other people."

"And where is he now?"

"He died. He left the house and the nursery to me. I took over the business because I didn't want to see it fold. I used to help him in the summer and I loved it. I wanted to do it myself."

It had been against everyone's advice. There was no future in it; she didn't have the education or the business background to make it a viable business. She'd never make enough money to live on.

She didn't care about the money. Ignoring everyone, she'd quit college in the middle of her master's degree in education. Her father had been outraged. Her sister, just out of law school at the time, had declared her mentally deficient. But that was nothing new. Suzanne had called her variations of the same thing as long as Jenny could remember.

Suzanne was four years older than Jenny. She was beautiful, smart, clever and bitchy. She was a promising lawyer now, stepping in their father's footsteps, working for a prestigious firm in Syracuse. She was the pride of their parents. Jenny didn't see much of Suzanne, which was just as well. Her parents lived a forty-five minute drive away and now and then she'd go home for Sunday dinner. On the surface everything was fine, but she knew her parents still did not approve of the way she lived. They could not forgive her for not getting her degree.

In a way everybody had been right. Her income was very low, but she managed. She had the house and the land and she grew most of her own food. She was independent, so her family would just have to adjust.

She didn't tell Kane about quitting college or about her brilliant sister. A man like him would very likely agree with her parents and her sister about the wisdom of what she had done.

She'd never been sorry. She was happy. She loved the freedom she had working for herself. She loved getting up in the morning and getting out into the fresh air, working with living green things. Spring blooms, summer scents, fall color—she would never get enough of all the beauty around her. She would feel like a caged animal within the four walls of an office or classroom.

"Have you ever thought of making a career of it?" he asked.

"A career?"

"Landscape architecture."

"No, not seriously."

"Why not?"

"It would take too many years and it costs too much money. I'm done sitting in overheated classrooms listening to theories and irrelevant lectures. Give me mud and a shovel and let me play."

"It's an investment in your future. You're still young. You should think about that."

"You sound like my father." She took a sip of coffee. "I'm happy doing what I'm doing. I don't see any reason to change my life." She looked outside. A yellow VW beetle mounted on gigantic tractor wheels rumbled past. Apparently she was not the only one who liked to play.

"Forgive me if I'm out of line," he said after a pause, "but in a small place like Guilford your business can only be marginal."

"Oh, it is," she said lightly, "but I manage. And you're right, you're out of line. It's none of your business."

"Ouch. My apologies." He smiled so disarmingly that it was hard not to smile back. He finished his coffee and sat back in his chair, studying her.

"That's quite a scratch you have there," he observed.

It sure was. A real battle scar. She fingered it gingerly. "I should have a matching one on the other side and I'd look like a jungle Indian with tribal scars."

He grinned. "I think your coloring is a bit off. Does it still hurt?"

"No, not really."

"I didn't mean to frighten you last night, you know. I thought you were a kid looking for trouble."

"It's all right."

"Am I forgiven?"

She made a face. "Okay, okay, you've forgiven."

He let out a big sigh, feigning relief. "Good." For a long moment his eyes held hers and warmth flooded into her cheeks. *This is ridiculous,* she thought. *What's happening to me?*

You know what's happening to you, her other self answered. *Here's this interesting man looking into your eyes and you're feeling all those delicious, dangerous stirrings. It's wonderful, it's exciting, and you know exactly what it means.*

"You know what I'm thinking of right now?" he asked, his gaze sliding lower and focusing on her mouth.

"No."

"Yes, you do. I'm thinking I'd like to kiss you."

Good Lord, he did speak his mind. "It's not allowed," she said lightly.

His eyebrows shot up. "Not allowed?"

"No kissing allowed in Sammy's Superduper Diner. There's a sign over the door."

He examined the door. "I see no sign."

"No? Gee, it was there just the other day."

He held her gaze and his eyes crinkled at the corners. "Well, I guess I'm out of luck."

"And I'm out of time. I'd better get back to my tomatoes." She put her napkin on the table and reached for her purse.

He fished some bills out of his jeans pocket. "Do you really have to get back to work or do you have time for a tour of the house?"

She felt herself tense. She didn't want to go to the house. *Maybe another time. I really should get back to work.* She swallowed the words. It would be childish to react like that just because she was disappointed at not getting the job. And of course she really did want to see the house; in all those years she'd never been inside it. She pushed her chair back and came to her feet. "I'd like that."

Besides, she told herself, why go back to work when you can be with him? A man like Kane Powell doesn't walk into your life every day. He was a little too presumptuous and much too sure of himself, but he had an undeniable charm and he certainly wasn't dull. There was something in his smile, in those warm brown eyes, that appealed to the romantic in her.

Only once before had a man made such an immediate impression on her. An instructor in college. She'd fallen for him hook, line and sinker. When she'd dropped out of college, he had dropped her. Driving forty-five minutes to see her wasn't worth the trouble when there were hundreds of female students right on campus.

The distance of years had given her a perspective, but at the time the disillusionment had devastated her. True love, she'd believed. True love as long as there were no challenges. Perfect love. Perfect as long as nothing marred the shiny surface of their happiness. It was the very perfection that ruined their relationship. After all, perfection is too fragile, too easily shattered. Now, three years later, the pain had faded and she understood it better. The bitterness had gone. Nothing was ever really perfect. Not nature, not the most beautiful rose, the greenest tree. She smiled at herself. Not even Kane Powell with his too-big nose.

Kane opened the door, put his arm around her shoulder and steered her out ahead of him. As the door closed behind him, his arm dropped back by his side again. It had been nothing but a casual touch, yet the firm contact of his hand on her shoulder seemed somehow oddly intimate.

A moment later they were driving noiselessly along the road. Azaleas in bloom everywhere, tulips, blossoming trees. The sun bathed everything in a shimmer of gold—the grass, the houses, the glossy green of trees. Cool air wafted in through the open window, fragrant with the scents of spring—moist earth and new leaves and delicate blooms. Kane gave her a quick, sideways glance, meeting her eyes.

"It's spring," he said, and there was a wealth of meaning in the simple statement.

Her heart turned over at the look in his eyes. "Yes," she returned, feeling a delicious sense of recklessness, "it's spring."

Chapter Three

The gate was open at the house and the car slid quietly up the long, circular driveway, coming to a smooth stop in front of the main door. It was a large, old colonial that had belonged to a prominent family for the last hundred and fifty years or so. An elderly, unmarried woman, the last of the direct family line, had lived in it alone for the past twenty years. After her death the house was inherited by a distant relative in Texas who had put it on the market.

Workmen were everywhere, stripping wallpaper, repairing floors and staircases and replacing rotten window frames.

"I'm not going to make many structural changes," Kane explained as they walked through the rooms. "I like the original layout. But we have to redo the wiring and modernize the plumbing."

Despite the clutter of ladders and tools and miscellaneous junk everywhere it was easy to see it was a house of style and character with its magnificent, curving staircase, high-ceilinged rooms and solid oak doors.

While Kane talked to the workmen, Jenny strolled around some more, examining the views from the different windows. In one of the smaller rooms she found a blue sleeping bag on the floor, an overnight bag and a pile of papers. Obviously, Kane had slept here last night. She visualized his big body relaxed and asleep, his face calm, eyes closed. She could feel herself grow warm. Good God, what's getting into me? she thought. Spring, that's what it was. All the juices flowing freely, including her own. And he knew it. Maybe he was playing games. He could be married, for all she knew.

"So, what do you think?" Kane was standing next to her, giving her an inquiring look.

She almost felt guilty standing there staring at his sleeping bag, as if he had caught her in some indecent act.

"It's going to be the showplace of Guilford," she stated.

He gave her a lopsided smile. "You think so?"

She nodded silently. *And I wish you'd let me do the grounds. I'd know what to do.* "Let's go outside," she suggested impulsively.

It had rained all through the night and the ground was saturated. Their sneakers squished through the wet soil as they walked around.

The grounds were overgrown with sumac, most of which would have to be dug up. The paths were hard to find, hidden by pachysandra and periwinkle growing rampant. Rosebushes were nothing but tangled masses of twisted, thorny branches which had sprouted in every direction. Ivy crept thick and green over a crumbling wall. Amid the confusion of greenery that had been growing without restraint for years, a few blue spruces reached up to the sky in mighty splendor.

"No matter what they say, don't let them cut down those spruces," she said.

He raised his brows in question. "Why not?"

"Look at them! They're some of the most beautiful trees around. One of my favorites, actually, along with Japanese maples and weeping willows. What are your favorites?"

He shook his head. "I've never thought about it. I just like trees. And bushes and flowers. And mountains and hills and deep dark forests."

She smiled. "You sound like a romantic."

"I am." Sparks of laughter danced in his eyes. He reached out and put his hands against her cheeks, cradling her head. His hands felt warm against her skin. His gaze lowered toward her mouth and her heart began to thud with loud, heavy beats. Then very slowly he moved his hand and his thumb softly brushed her mouth, gently tracing the edge of her lips, then settled between them as she parted them slightly.

She stood very still, afraid to break the spell, afraid he'd release her. He removed his thumb, smiling. "You have a beautiful mouth," he said softly. Slowly he moved his face toward her, closer and closer until his lips touched hers. The impact of his touch made her blood rush hot and fast through her body and her lips parted instinctively as his mouth caressed hers. It was a tender kiss, soft, but utterly sensuous. She could not pull herself away. She felt heady with his nearness, the feel of his hands and mouth, the scent of him.

Her hands slid across his back, delighting in the feel of the strong, hard muscles under her fingers. A soft sigh escaped her and suddenly his kiss deepened as he drew her closer, pressing himself against her, and the heat of his body ignited hers and fire leaped through her.

He released her suddenly, heaving a sigh and raking his hand through his hair. She noticed the slight tremor in his hand and the tension in his eyes. But then, as he looked at her, a smile tilted his mouth and his eyes softened.

She averted her gaze, embarrassed by this unexpected display of passion, by her flushed face and pounding heart. They could probably hear it all the way to New York. With an effort she calmed herself. "Why did you do that?"

He laughed. "Because I wanted to. I told you I wanted to."

"Do you always go around kissing people in gardens?"

"Only the ones I like."

"Should I be flattered?" She couldn't help smiling a little.

He nodded. "Immensely. I haven't kissed anybody in a garden in years." He leaned his face close to hers, looking into her eyes. "And tell me, do you have fantasies other than about landscaping gardens?"

Yes, she answered silently, about being swept off my feet by a man with warm brown eyes and gentle fingers.

"That's a very personal question," she said. "It's not good manners to ask a woman about her fantasies."

He grinned disarmingly. "I know."

There was a sudden rustle in the undergrowth, then something small and brownish-gray scurried past their feet and up the trunk of a big maple tree.

"Was that a squirrel?" he asked, staring up into the green canopy of leaves.

"Yes. You've got rabbits here, too, and chipmunks and woodchucks and who knows what other wildlife."

"Good, I like that."

"Mmm, I wouldn't be too quick saying that. Rabbits wreak havoc in a vegetable garden."

"I don't think I'll have one. I imagine you can supply me with whatever I'll need."

She gave him a quick, suspicious glance, but his face was innocent, as had been his voice.

"I want lots of roses in this garden," he said, glancing around. "Big bushes. All colors. Red and white and yellow and pink."

Yes, she thought. *Yes. And I know exactly where to put them.* The smile faded from her face and all joy evaporated. There was an ache inside her, a sense of loss and sorrow. All those ideas that had been germinating in her head would find no reality. Working outside or in the greenhouse, she'd often daydreamed about what she would do with the Cleever house grounds, visualizing all the various possibilities. Now someone else would redesign the grounds and nothing would be the way she had pictured it in her mind.

"What's wrong?"

She shrugged lightly. "Nothing."

"Yes there is." He stopped walking and scrutinized her face, with a frown. "Something wrong with roses?"

"No. They'd be just right."

"Then why do you look like somebody just died?"

"Oh, for heaven's sake!" She sighed. "All right, I'll tell you." She bit her lip, not sure she really should be doing this. "I'm disappointed. I've thought about this place a lot in the last couple of years. I kept thinking about all the things I could do with it. It's been my fantasy to landscape this garden. I have so many ideas. I'd hoped... Well, anyway, I'm not blaming you personally." She smiled wryly, giving a light shrug. "At least I'm trying not to. I do understand why you'd rather have a professional company take on the job. I'm not qualified and I've never done anything as big as this."

"It's a pretty big job for an amateur."

Amateur!

The word had a bitter taste and suddenly anger rushed through her. Amateur! She turned away abruptly, jamming her hands into the pockets of her jeans and walked on. He followed her, putting his hand on her shoulder and making her stop.

"What's the matter with you?" he demanded.

"Nothing is the matter with me!"

His eyes narrowed. "I've got too much money invested in this house, Jennifer. You have to understand."

She forced down the anger. "I do understand."

She was acting like a spoiled brat who couldn't have what she wanted, yet she couldn't help herself. Maybe it wasn't really that. She felt humiliated, rejected. She wanted him to know she was capable of landscaping his garden, she wanted more than anything for him to respect her and value her capabilities. But there was no way she knew to convince him. She was nothing more than an amateur with a green thumb. It was the truth, and there was nothing wrong with that.

"Please, don't be angry with me," he said.

It wasn't fair for her to take her frustrations out on him. He didn't owe her the job. He owed her nothing.

"I'm sorry," she said. "I was being childish and immature."

He smiled crookedly. "I'm sorry, too."

They were at the far end of the grounds and silently they began to make their way back to the house.

"What kind of garden do you want?" she asked at last, breaking the silence. "What do you want to do with it?"

He looked puzzled. "I want it to be beautiful. What do you mean?"

"A garden isn't just for looking beautiful. It is a space to use. Are you going to put a pool in? A hot tub, tennis courts?"

He looked pained. "Good Lord, no."

Jenny stopped to examine a dead-looking branch on a gnarled apple tree. The dry twigs snapped easily between her fingers. No green inside, no juices flowing through the branch to make it sprout new leaves.

"What about a play area for children?" she asked. "Swing set, sandbox, jungle gym, that sort of thing." She was aware that she held her breath waiting for an answer. A shadow crossed his face and then the smile was gone from his eyes. She saw the naked pain, fleeting, but undeniable and her heart contracted.

"No." His voice was toneless. "I don't have a family. No wife, no children."

His reaction, the bleak look on his face, was not what she had expected and for a moment she was at a loss for words. She could not ask what was wrong.

"I'm sorry," she said softly. "I didn't mean..."

"It's all right." He touched her hand briefly and gave a lopsided smile, but still the sadness was there in his eyes. "I'll take you back now so you can finish planting your tomatoes."

"Jenny, I need a big favor." Mary's voice sounded vaguely panicked, which was worrying. Mary was not the panicky type. They'd been friends ever since Jenny had moved to Guilford, and Jenny liked Mary's calm, down-to-earth nature.

Jenny pressed the phone between shoulder and ear and went on peeling the onion. Her eyes were watering and she sniffed. "Shoot."

"My babysitter broke her wrist, can you believe it? Tonight of all nights? And we've got to go to that dinner tonight. Remember I told you about that dinner? It's important."

"So bring Justin here."

"Oh, Jenny, you wouldn't mind?"

"Nope. Not in the least. I'll enjoy having him." Justin was eight months old, a calm, happy baby. She wouldn't mind at all.

"You weren't planning anything?"

Jenny laughed. "When was the last time I had something planned, Mary?"

Mary sighed. "I know. We've got to do something about that you know."

"Don't worry about me. When will you bring him over?"

"About seven. Is that all right?"

"Fine. I'll see you then."

Jenny hung up the phone and started chopping the onion, then heard a car arrive. Moments later Kane's head, sporting the ever-present leather cap, appeared in front of the open window.

"What's for dinner?"

Her eyes were watering and his face looked blurry. "Rice and lentils."

"Rice and lentils. Fascinating. Is there enough for two?"

"Are you inviting yourself to dinner?"

"How perceptive of you! Are you crying?"

She sniffed. "Yes. Buckets."

"You need a shoulder?"

She slid the chopped onions into the frying pan and tossed the knife in the sink. "I'd prefer some tissues, but the box is in the bathroom."

"I'll get it." His head disappeared and a moment later he entered the kitchen, walked straight through and came back with the tissues.

"Good heavens," he said, looking at her, "they look almost real."

"Of course they're real. Genuine 24-karat tears." She wiped her eyes.

He leaned lazily against the counter, arms crossed in front of his chest. "Am I making a nuisance of myself?"

She turned on the tap and washed her hands. Good question, she thought. "Maybe, maybe not," she answered. "It all depends."

He grinned, tossing his cap on a chair. "What I like is a clear answer."

She searched around for the towel. "Stir the onions for me, please."

"Only if I can stay for dinner."

"If you can live without meat, you're most welcome."

He picked up the wooden spoon and stirred the onions. "Are you a genuine vegetarian?"

Jenny opened a jar of tomatoes she had canned the previous fall. "No, I just pretend a lot. I do it out of poverty. When chicken is 49 cents a pound I eat chicken."

"You don't seem to be suffering."

"I bet I'm healthier than most. If you're interested in a lecture on the benefits of eating less meat, let me know. Move over a little, I need to put these in." She poured half the jar of tomatoes into the frying pan, then added the cooked lentils. "Keep stirring. Do you cook for yourself?"

"I do a great pepper steak."

"Heart attack city."

"My doctor says my blood cholesterol is just fine, thank you."

She grinned. "I love pepper steak."

He grinned back at her. "Are you inviting yourself for dinner?"

"Me?" She feigned indignation. "I'd never do that. I'd never be so—uh—brazen."

He laughed. "Brazen? Nice word. Well, how about if I properly invite you to come into the city one Friday night? I'll cook you a steak at my place and afterward we can go see a play or concert or whatever you like."

And after that it would be too late to take her all the way back to Guilford.

She looked up. "Where will I stay?"

One corner of his mouth tilted. "At my place."

She stirred the lentils, not sure what her reply should be.

"What are you thinking?" His hand slipped under her hair and rested on the nape of her neck. Unsuccessfully she tried to quell the surge of electricity that sparked through her. It was frightening what one touch of this man could do to her nervous system. He stirred in her so many hidden yearnings, such a restless, feverish desire.

"You know what I'm thinking."

He reached out and took the wooden spoon from her fingers and turned her around to face him. He rested his forearms loosely on her shoulders and held her gaze.

"I...like you very much. I like being with you. You must know that."

She didn't answer. There was no need to.

"And I think," he went on, "that you're feeling the same way."

Her heart thundered in her chest. "Yes."

He smiled. "But there's a 'but' isn't there?"

"You're going too fast," she said almost regretfully. "This is a slow country town, not New York City. I'm afraid the speed makes me dizzy."

He laughed. "I'll step on the brakes. I'm asking you to dinner and an evening out. No strings attached. I want your company in whatever way is comfortable for you. How's that?"

She couldn't suppress a smile. "Very clever. Where will I sleep?"

"At my place."

"In the bathtub?"

"If you like. But I do have a guest room. My bed is the best though—big and comfortable and it has me in it."

"Your brakes are bad, Mr. Powell."

He laughed. "Will you come?"

"I'd love to." An evening out in New York City—something to look forward to. She hadn't been out for ages, apart from a movie at the local theater which was overrun with necking teenagers and awash in popcorn and candy wrappers. She couldn't even remember the last time she'd been to New York.

I've got nothing to wear! she thought in a panic. *All I've got is that awful yellow dress that makes me look like an overripe grapefruit.* Well, she'd have to figure something out. He was still looking at her and she hastily stepped back. "The food's going to burn."

She spiced up the lentils with some dried herbs and checked the rice. "We can eat now. Sit down and I'll get you a plate. What would you like to drink? Water or milk?"

"Water, please. So, how do we eat this?"

"You pour the lentils over the rice, like spaghetti sauce, and then you sprinkle some of the grated cheese over it and dig in."

They served themselves out of the pans and began to eat. "It's good," Kane said after a few mouthfuls.

"I'm glad you think so."

After they were finished he helped her do the dishes, drying, while she washed. He seemed quite domesticated, which wasn't bad. A car crunched up the gravel driveway and she peered out the kitchen window to see.

"Oh, it's Justin."

"You were expecting company?" Kane's voice was carefully bland.

She smiled at him. "Yes. Sorry, I forgot to tell you."

"None of my business, is it? I'll get out of your way."

"Oh, that's not necessary. I'm sure Justin won't mind at all." There was a knock on the door. "Come in!"

"I can't!" It was Mary's voice, low and frustrated. "I've got my hands full!"

"Just a sec!" Jenny noticed Kane's puzzled expression and gave him a wicked grin as she opened the door.

Mary stepped inside, her tall, skinny frame weighted down with a variety of articles, like a street peddler in Calcutta. Her left hip supported Justin, who seemed in imminent danger of sliding off. Her right shoulder looked strained under the weight of her purse and a large diaper bag, and one hand clutched a portable bed.

Jenny took the baby from her and Mary dropped the various pieces of luggage on the floor, her green eyes widening as she noticed Kane, who was watching the scene with an amused grin.

"Jenny!" Mary wailed reprovingly. "You should have told me! I asked you if you had any plans!"

"I didn't, and I don't." Jenny waved her hand casually at Kane. "He just strolled in unannounced and invited himself for dinner." She gave them both a sweet smile. "Now, let me introduce you. Mary, this is Kane Powell, the new owner of the Cleever house. Kane, meet my friend, Mary Kingsley."

They shook hands. Mary studied Kane with blatant curiosity. Like the rest of her, her face was thin and long, the curly brown hair standing out like a halo around it.

Justin squirmed in Jenny's arms and gave a wail of outrage when his mother did not take him back.

Mary moved to the door. "I haven't even fed him yet. He's probably starving. There's food in the bag—a bottle and a jar of spinach, his favorite."

Jenny made a face. "Spinach?"

Mary rolled her eyes. "I'm going to have a real Popeye on my hands." She picked up her purse and opened the door. She looked pained when Justin began to howl. "Oh, my, I hope he won't ruin your evening."

"Go, go," Jenny urged, trying for dear life to hang on to the wriggling child. "We'll be fine. Have a good time, okay?"

The door closed and Kane reached for Justin. "Here, let me hold him."

She handed him over. "I can't believe how strong he is for such a little thing."

"Must be the spinach." Kane put his arms firmly around the small body and Justin stopped wailing and looked at Kane. His little hand shot out and grabbed Kane's nose.

"Yeah, I know it's beautiful, but you can't have it." He pried the small hand loose and Justin gave a howl of frustration.

"All right, little man, let's calm down. We'll find you something to eat, okay?" His tone was soft and soothing. "Seven o'clock and you haven't had your dinner yet. It's a cryin' shame, I know, I know."

Justin suddenly grew calm and stared up at Kane in wide-eyed wonder.

"Thank you," Kane said solemnly. "I always like people who listen to reason. Now, let's see if we can't find you some food."

Jenny had been watching the exchange with fascination and she grinned at Kane. "I'll get it." She rummaged through the diaper bag and extracted the bottle and the jar of spinach. She frowned as she put them on the table.

"What's the matter?"

"I'm wondering which first."

"The spinach. If he gets the milk first he won't eat the spinach."

She grinned. "The voice of experience."

He looked down at the baby's face and did not reply, and for a terrible tension-laden moment she knew she'd touched a raw nerve. She took the bottle and put it in a pan of hot water to warm, her lightheartedness suddenly vanished.

"I'll take him and feed him," she said quietly.

"I'll do it. Just open the jar for me and give me a spoon."

She did as he requested, then sat down at the table and watched as he fed the baby, deftly evading the small arm as it grasped for the spoon, keeping up a running conversation about ships and airplanes full of spinach and other ridiculous nonsense. Justin was obviously hungry and gobbled up the vile-looking green stuff in no time at all. He cried with frustrated indignation when the jar was empty.

"Hey, just a minute," Kane said, "there's more. What do you want? We've got some lentils and rice left over, or how about . . . okay, okay, milk it is. Why didn't you say so before you spoke?"

Jenny laughed and handed him the warm bottle. Justin began to guzzle hungrily as soon as Kane pushed the nipple into his open mouth. He was comfortably cradled in the crook of Kane's arm, and as Jenny watched she was well aware of the ease with which Kane handled the baby.

He must have a child of his own, she thought. *But he told me he didn't have children.*

Before the bottle was empty, Justin was overcome by fatigue and his tiny eyelids began to droop sleepily.

Kane put the bottle on the table and for a long moment he just sat there looking down at the baby's face, a mixture of emotions in his eyes—tenderness and longing and an unmistakable sadness. Finally he looked up and smiled at Jenny.

"He's finished for the day, I should say. Here, you take him and I'll get his bed ready. Where do you want it?"

She frowned, considering the possibilities. "My office has the most room, I guess."

She hugged the soft warm body to her as she followed Kane with the bed. Moments later the baby was peacefully asleep and they quietly left the room, leaving the door ajar.

"You want some coffee?" she asked.

"Please." He straddled a chair and looked at her appraisingly. "Would you mind if I asked you a personal question?"

"You asked me one this afternoon in your garden. One a day is my quota."

"I did?" He looked innocent. "Ah, yes, the one about the fantasies. But I didn't get an answer. What happened?"

"The squirrel saved me."

"Right. Too bad. But since I didn't get an answer, it doesn't count."

She put water in the kettle and turned on the stove. "All right, shoot."

"Am I correct in assuming that there is no man in your life? And I speak romantically here, to be perfectly clear."

"Yes."

He grinned. "That was easy."

"And what about you?"

"I'm a monk."

"Yeah, you look like one."

"You don't believe me?"

"Not for a minute."

He looked wounded. "Why not?"

"You work in New York, wear expensive clothes, deal with wealthy people. You drive a Lincoln Continental. You travel all over the world, staying—no doubt—in posh hotels. I imagine your apartment is something out of a magazine. I don't need a calculator to add it all up, Mr. Powell. You're a monk, you say? Sure. Tell me another fairy tale."

"How am I going to convince you?"

"I don't know. Does it matter?"

"Of course it matters." He frowned, studying her. "If I tell you that there's no woman in my life, and hasn't been for some time now, will you believe me?"

There was no way to know if he was telling the truth. He could be one of the greatest con men alive, but she wasn't experienced enough to recognize an expert. Yet for some reason she felt she could trust him. Maybe because I'm stupid and *want* to believe him, she told herself cynically. She gave him an assessing look, hesitating.

"I'd like to, but . . ."

"But what?"

She shrugged. "I'm not exactly your type."

His eyebrows shot up. "And what is my type?"

"Oh . . . sexy, slinky and sophisticated, not to mention glamorous and gorgeous."

He laughed. "And you, poor Cinderella, are nothing but a small-town country girl who likes to get her hands dirty."

She smiled sweetly. "Something like that." But not quite. She'd certainly not grown up as a country girl. She was quite familiar with the lifestyle of the well-to-do, the influential.

She just didn't care for it very much; she'd never liked the sort of individuals who peopled her parents' world—out to impress everybody, out to make a buck, out to exercise power and influence and to hell with everybody else.

The kettle began to shriek. Quickly she turned off the burner, then reached for a spoon and the jar of instant coffee. "How much?"

"Make it strong."

"So," she said casually, spooning coffee into the mugs, "what's wrong with you?"

"Wrong with me?" He sounded amazed.

"A man like you doesn't walk around unattached without good reason. It makes a woman wonder." She turned to look at him, when he didn't answer immediately.

"I hadn't thought about that," he said at last, his voice level. "I suppose I have a good reason."

And then she remembered what he had said that afternoon. *I don't have a family. No wife, no children.* She remembered seeing the raw pain in his eyes. Oh, damn, she thought, why didn't I think before I spoke?

"Sorry," she said quietly. "I shouldn't have asked that."

"It's all right, Jennifer." He paused. "I was married once. We had a little boy. They both died within a year."

"Oh, my God," she whispered, stricken.

"Kevin died of meningitis when he was only two years old," he went on. "Less than a year later Anne and I were in Italy, skiing. She had an accident and was critically injured. She was in a coma for more than two months before she died." His voice was calm, as if merely reciting facts, but she could see the agony mirrored in his eyes and his hands were balled into fists, the knuckles white.

Her mouth went dry. She couldn't think of anything to say.

"I wasn't interested in women for a long time," he said after a pause, looking at her steadily. "Eventually I had another relationship, but it turned out wrong. Probably because I wasn't ready for it to be right, if that makes any sense." He shrugged. "I think that subconsciously I wanted what I had before, and of course there's no way for that to happen. It isn't realistic and it isn't fair to a woman, of course."

She looked at him wordlessly, and she felt awkward and inept standing there.

"Make the coffee," he said gently, smiling at her. "And don't look so stricken."

She poured water into the mugs, aware of his eyes following her moves. She wondered why he had confided in her. Something was happening. A silken thread of emotion was weaving itself between them, fragile and intangible. She would have to be careful, very careful.

She set the mugs on the table and found a bag of cookies before sitting down. "I hope I don't offend your palate by offering you Oreo cookies. I don't do much baking, although I can do some pretty sophisticated stuff with strawberries when they're in season."

"As a kid, Oreo cookies were my favorite. I used to take them apart and lick off the filling before I ate the cookies."

She pushed the bag toward him. "Be my guest. Lick all you want."

He laughed. "I outgrew the habit."

"Too bad. I was looking forward to watching you. Tell me about yourself. Where did you grow up? How did you end up in the import business? Stuff like that."

"Supposedly I was born in Boston."

"Supposedly?" She licked a crumb off her lip.

"That's what my birth certificate says. But my elder sister said it wasn't true. She used to tell me I was a foundling and she'd discovered me in the backyard behind the forsythia bushes. My mother always denied it, but my sister insisted and on numerous occasions she pointed out the exact place where she'd found me, elaborating on such details as what I was wearing and the cardboard box I was lying in. A packing carton for chicken noodle soup, it was. I've always hated chicken noodle soup. She's six years older than I am and I believed her for a long time."

"That's cruel!"

He grinned. "Don't worry. When I grew older and smarter I made her pay many times over."

"Maybe she was jealous."

"No doubt about it. She'd been an only child for a long time and when I came along it spoiled her little world."

"Do you get along with her now?"

"We're the best of friends, which is easy when you live miles apart. I have another sister two years younger than I. My parents still live in Boston. When I finished college, I packed a backpack and wandered around the world for two years, working at odd jobs and staying in various places when the staying was good. That's how I got interested in different types of art and how I got the idea of importing it, to make a long story short." He took a swallow of coffee and studied her with narrowed eyes. "You know, I like looking at you."

She glowered at him. "If this is the start of a seduction routine, forget it."

He laughed out loud. "Boy, are you suspicious! I like you better all the time."

And it was more than liking, Kane admitted as he lay in his sleeping bag that night. There was something real and honest about her. No pretense. No excuses for the mess in her kitchen or the food she cooked. Instant coffee and Oreo cookies for dessert. It made him smile.

You know what I hate most about my work? she'd asked earlier that evening. She'd tilted her head, her hair swinging forward over her shoulder. He could still see her eyes—wistful, a little wary, as if she weren't quite sure if she should tell him.

"No, what?"

"Thinning seedlings. They all look so brave and beautiful and so terribly eager." She'd smiled a little, a funny smile that reflected in her eyes, as if she thought she'd sound silly and sentimental but wasn't about to apologize for it. "It seems...sinful, somehow, destroying all that hopeful green, just ripping them out and throwing them away."

He hadn't thought her silly.

He sighed and stirred restlessly in his sleeping bag, staring out of the open window.

She was suspicious of him, despite the obvious electricity between them—or maybe because of it. She probably wondered if he was looking for a fling or another relationship that wouldn't work out because he didn't really want it to. He rubbed his forehead. It was the last thing he wanted.

A few years ago he hadn't thought he'd ever get over Anne's and Kevin's deaths. And he probably never would completely. But the edges of the pain had dulled. Yet now and then, unexpectedly, something would remind him and the grief would hit him like a knife.

Alone again, he had worked harder than ever, traveling almost constantly and spending very little time at home. He could not bear to be alone in the place where everything reminded him of the two people he'd loved most in the world. He'd moved into another apartment, bought new furniture and tried to adjust to his bachelor status again. It hadn't been easy. No matter how far and long he traveled, his loneliness followed him like a dark shadow. There was no place that gave him peace.

The moonlight shone through the curtainless windows. It made him think of the times he'd slept on deserted beaches in the far corners of the world. Sometimes he wished he could go back to those times, be young again, without cares and without pain. He wondered if Jennifer would like sleeping on a beach. He wished she were with him now, her small, soft body nestled against him in the sleeping bag, looking at the moon.

No, not looking at the moon. He groaned and closed his eyes, trying to push her out of his mind. It was a lost cause. Her face kept intruding in his dreams, the blue eyes, the proud tilt of her chin. He could feel again her trembling mouth when he had kissed her, her breasts as they had brushed against his chest. He sat up with a start, his heart pounding. "My God," he muttered to the moon, "I'm like a lovesick adolescent."

Sunday morning the refrigerator died. It gave up the ghost with a sudden shudder, followed by an ominous silence. With a sick feeling in her stomach, Jenny stared at the relic. Last year it had given her problems and Billy James had fixed it for her, saying the thing was ready for the scrap heap. It was over twenty years old, a museum piece, and it certainly was no wonder it had finally quit. The poor thing deserved to rest in peace, but where was she going to get the money to buy a new one? She had a little over six hundred dollars in the bank and that was the grand total of her net worth. A refrigerator would take care of most of it.

You knew this was going to happen sooner or later, she told herself. *You know you're not running a viable business. Just eating is not enough these days.* Everybody had told her so and she'd stubbornly refused to listen.

She took a deep breath. Well, as long as she wasn't going hungry, she wasn't defeated. She'd check around to see if there wasn't a secondhand one she could buy, and if that failed she'd call Sears and see what they had on sale this week.

Later that afternoon she went home to her parents' house for Sunday dinner and listened to Suzanne talking fancy lawyer talk with her father and watched David meticulously cutting his meat in tiny pieces before starting to eat. Not so classy, after all, she thought with malicious satisfaction.

She didn't like David. He was a snob and a phony. His father was a laborer working on building sites and David talked about him in a condescending fashion that made Jenny bristle. The man had fed and clothed him and put a roof over his head and now he wasn't good enough anymore for Sonny Boy, who was making it big in real estate. She couldn't understand why Suzanne put up with him. She looked with distaste at his handsome face. He looked almost pretty, like a woman, with long dark lashes, a full mouth and a perfectly chiseled nose. It made her think of Kane's nose, too big, with a bump in the middle. Much more interesting, a nose like that. It made her smile at her mashed potatoes.

"What are you grinning at?" David looked at her with haughty amusement, as if she were a child.

"You wouldn't understand," she said sweetly.

"Try me."

"Would you hand me the pepper, please?" she asked politely.

Suzanne looked gorgeous in a simple but fashionable blue dress. She had great taste, Jenny had to admit. Suzanne asked how business was. Jenny said it was going very well. The tomatoes looked good. The peas were doing well, as were the lettuce and spinach. Suzanne didn't care about peas and lettuce, but since she was asking Jenny figured she might as well tell her. She didn't mention the demise of the refrigerator. She had the sneaking suspicion that Suzanne was waiting for disaster to strike her just so she could tell her "I told you so!"

Well, it'll take more than a refrigerator to do me in, Jenny thought as she sipped the last of her wine.

It was still early when she drove home in the old red pickup. Driving past the Cleever house, she glanced down the drive but saw no sign of the gray Continental. Kane had probably gone back to New York for the week.

But he had not. He came by on Monday and accepted her offer of a cup of coffee. She was happy having him in her kitchen; strangely, he seemed to belong there, looking quite at home with his long legs stretched out comfortably under the table, his jacket thrown casually over the back of a chair. He was taking off a week, maybe two, he said, to deal with the house and make sure everything was going the way he intended it to go.

It was a busy week and she didn't see him often during the day, but at night they'd share a meal, see a movie or talk. It was the talking she liked best, listening to his voice and the things he told her about himself. She liked looking at his face, seeing all the different emotions flit across it as he talked. She liked watching his hands, wishing he would touch her.

Sometimes he would touch her—take her hand or move a strand of hair away from her face, but he made no attempt to kiss her. Now and then she'd catch him watching her and she sensed in him a tension that seemed to echo her own.

In the back of her mind there were always the questions. What about his wife and child? Had he loved his wife?

What kind of woman had she been? Why did a man like Kane want to move to a little place like Guilford?

Saturday was one of the busiest days she'd had that spring and she felt dead tired as she got into the shower after she'd closed up. For a long time she stood in the warm water, trying to revive herself. With a towel wrapped around herself, she walked out into the hall to go to her room.

She stopped, frowning, sniffing the air. What was that smell? Pizza? She walked toward the kitchen, stopping in the door when she saw Kane sitting at the table looking through a seed catalog. A bottle of wine stood on the counter.

He looked up and a smile warmed his face as he saw her standing there. "Well, hello there," he said softly.

She clutched the towel to her, her heart beating erratically. Oh, God, she thought, this is ridiculous. My heart is not going to hold out if I keep giving it such a workout every time I see him.

"I thought I smelled pizza," she said unsteadily, uncomfortably aware of being naked under the towel; knowing he knew it, too.

"You did. It's in the oven keeping warm."

"I didn't know you were here."

"I took the liberty of letting myself in when you didn't answer the door. I heard the shower."

"I'll get dressed."

"Don't." He came to his feet. "Come here, Jennifer."

Her legs wouldn't move. She shook her head, watching him as he came toward her. She held out a hand as if to ward him off, and he took it, tugging at it to draw her close. He slid his hands over her bare shoulders, up under her hair. His eyes held hers and she felt like drowning in their depths.

His mouth was warm and urgent, and desire rushed through her like hot wine.

She tore her head away, still clutching at the towel. "No," she said huskily, "I'm getting dressed."

Chapter Four

In the bedroom she ripped off the towel and flung it to the floor. Hastily she pulled on some jeans and a shirt, her fingers trembling as she wrestled with the buttons.

She took a steadying breath. You're not surprised, are you? she chided herself. Standing there wrapped in a towel you can expect a red-blooded male to come after you. You were an open invitation.

She brushed out her hair, staring at herself in the mirror, seeing her flushed face and the unfamiliar glitter in her eyes. She let out a deep sigh. She wasn't exactly cold-blooded herself and Kane Powell certainly had his attractions. She groaned, closing her eyes. There was no reason to fool herself. It was more than just attraction.

Having found a reasonable measure of composure, she went back to the kitchen.

"I'm starving," she said, trying to sound casual.

"Dinner's coming up." He opened the oven and extracted the pizza. He set it on the table and started cutting it into wedges. "How about pouring some wine?" he asked calmly.

"Sure." Relieved, she found some glasses and picked up the wine bottle.

"I see you got your fridge," he commented, gesturing at the new Kenmore. In its shiny splendor it looked rather out of place in the tacky old kitchen. She'd called every imaginable place looking for a secondhand one. She'd not been successful, but she had found one on sale.

"It came yesterday." Writing the check had been a painful business. Her fingers had practically cramped up in the effort. *Please don't let me need a root canal,* she'd prayed as she signed her name. Her medical insurance didn't cover dental care.

They watched a movie on TV while they ate pizza and drank wine, and she began to feel pleasantly sleepy from the hard day's work and the warm glow of the wine in her blood.

"Hey, you're falling asleep!" Kane nudged her gently.

She opened her eyes and quickly straightened her back. "I had a busy day." She shook the hair out of her face.

"Shall I leave?"

"No, stay." Her hand shot out involuntarily and took his. "The movie isn't even finished." She tried to pull her hand away, but he took it in a firm grip and held it.

"Come a little closer," he said. He put his arm around her shoulders and held her close. Her body tensed with the effort to keep calm. She didn't feel calm.

"Relax," he whispered.

"I'm trying to!"

He looked into her face and she noticed the glint of amusement in his eyes. His right hand came out and she felt the warm pressure of it on her left breast. A tingling sensation spiralled through her and she sat very still, barely able to breathe, willing her heart to calm down. His hand stirred on her breast.

"Your heart—am I doing that?"

"No! It's the movie. It's scaring me to death."

"It's a comedy."

"I guess I don't get it."

He laughed softly. "Liar." He drew her closer, so her head rested against his shoulder. His hand was still on her breast, his face close against hers. She felt the warmth of his breath against her cheek, felt the sweet excitement rise inside her, and she didn't want to fight and spoil it. For a long time they sat together without moving, then she took a deep breath and pulled away from him.

"I'm going to make some coffee."

She leaned against the kitchen counter, waiting for the water to boil. She was acting like a frightened virgin, and it annoyed her. She stared unseeingly at the kettle, wondering how she would deal with her jumpy nerves and volatile emotions. Kane Powell had succeeded in sweeping her off her feet and she'd lost her balance. He wanted her and she wanted him, there was no denying that; but she wasn't about to jump into bed with a man she hardly knew. Such brave, virtuous words, she chided herself, especially standing here in the relative safety of the kitchen.

By the time the coffee was made she had herself under control again. Squaring her shoulders, she picked up the tray and carried it back to the living room, where Kane was still watching the movie.

"What happened?" she asked.

"The daughter stole all her mother's jewelry and then the lover—the mother's lover—came to the daughter's apartment to get it back at gunpoint, but in the meantime the father and his boyfriend decided to..."

"Oh, God," Jenny groaned. "Turn it off."

"Great idea." He leaped to his feet and switched off the set, coming back to sit down next to her on the couch. "I'd much rather hear about your family, actually. You know you haven't told me much, except about your grandfather and how you spent your free time with him here. What about your parents, your sister?"

He had told her about his family. His father was a surgeon and his mother a ballet teacher. His elder sister was married and had two bratty children who constantly fought with each other; his younger sister taught English at Columbia University.

"Well," she began lightly, "my father is a lawyer. My sister is a lawyer. My mother is the Wicked Witch of the West and I play in the mud."

There was a short pause as he scrutinized her closely. "And they expected you to go into law, too?"

"Oh, no," she said breezily, "they're very broad-minded. They would have settled for neurosurgery or biochemical research."

"They don't approve of you running the nursery?"

"They're very ambitious people."

"But you are not?"

She shook her head. "Nope. I'm making an honest living and I'm doing what I like doing. I don't want the life my parents live. I couldn't take all the wheeling and dealing, the high-powered finagling that goes on in my father's profession. I don't want to end up like my mother." She gave a half smile. "Is there something wrong with wanting this? I like growing plants and flowers, working outside, not having anyone to answer to."

"I certainly can understand that. I'm not good with superiors, never was."

"You know, I wake up every morning and feel happy about it—well, almost every morning. I get dressed and go out first thing and just walk around the place and down the road a couple of miles. Just to look at the sky and listen to the early morning sounds and to get my body going. I like it most in the summer when the sun is just coming up and everything is very still. It's the most peaceful, joyful feeling. Then I go back, have coffee, some breakfast and plan my day. There's no rush. I'm my own boss. I like it; it's the way I want it.''

''What were you doing before you took over the nursery?''

''I was in graduate school.''

''Majoring in what?''

''Making Mom and Dad happy.''

''Ah, I see. And did you make them happy?''

''I dropped out.''

He nodded. ''Making Mom and Dad Happy courses are the most difficult ones there are.''

''Absolutely. It's too bad for my parents, though.'' She sighed regretfully. ''I really feel for them. I've always been such a disappointment to them. They don't like me being here, doing what I'm doing. My sister—you should meet my sister. She's gorgeous, brilliant. She was always set up as an example. She's very smart. She finished high school a year ahead of everybody. She breezed through college and law school. Everybody expected me to be just like her. All the aunts and uncles and friends and neighbors. 'Are you going to be just as smart as your sister?' they'd ask before I even started school. 'Are you going to be a lawyer just like your daddy and Suzanne?' Suzanne wanted to be a lawyer like my father since she was ten or something. I never knew what I wanted to be when I grew up, but everybody seemed to have their own ideas.'' She sighed melodramatically. ''All those expectations, weighing like a ton of bricks on my poor little head.''

"I can imagine. No wonder you're short."

She laughed. "That's terrible." She paused. "I used to wish I were Pippi Longstocking."

"Pippi what?"

"Pippi Longstocking. Haven't you ever heard of Pippi Longstocking?"

"I'm afraid not, but do enlighten me."

"She's a character in a children's book. It's Swedish originally, the book and the author I mean. Pippi had no parents and she lived all alone in this ramshackle old house with her horse and her monkey, Mr. Nilsson. She did exactly as she pleased because there was nobody to tell her what to do and what not to do. She didn't even go to school. Her mother died when she was little and her father got lost at sea, but she believed he was now king of a cannibal island. Pippi had it made. She was my heroine. I wouldn't have minded at all if my father had been king on a cannibal island. As a matter of fact, I think he'd be perfect." She grinned. "Not having a sister seemed bliss, but I had a little trouble with wishing my mother dead, even when I was angry. I felt guilty even considering it, and at night I'd pray my little heart out for forgiveness. Then I'd go right back to fantasizing what it would be like to live all alone and not have to go to school and talk back to adults and wear whatever I wanted. My mother used to dress us up like little dolls, all frills and ruffles and lace, and ribbons in our hair. I hated it."

"What did Pippi do for money?"

Jenny laughed out loud. "The practical businessman speaking. Well, Pippi had a treasure chest full of coins and jewelry. Stuff left over from her days at sea with her father, I think." She sighed. "That was my whole problem. I didn't have a treasure chest, so I couldn't run away and live on my own. But I had great plans for when I grew up. I used to say

I was going to work in the ice cream store so I could eat ice cream all day. That upset everybody. I liked that. When I was a teenager, I told them I was going to go to New York and work as a dancer in a nightclub."

Kane grinned. "I'll bet that didn't please them too much either."

"Oh, my parents didn't believe me for a minute, but they didn't understand why I was being so rebellious either." She sighed. "I worked my head off in school and all I got were B's. They kept saying I could get A's if I tried harder. After all, Suzanne got straight A's and I was smart enough to do the same. When I didn't measure up, they lost interest. Now they treat me like the village idiot."

"That bad, huh?"

"Well, almost." She grimaced. "My mother keeps bringing me food and telling me I should wash my dishes and clean my windows and cut my hair." She jumped up from the couch and stood by the window, hands clenched, forehead pressed against the cold glass. "God, I hate it!" she said in a choked voice.

He came up behind her, putting his arms around her waist. "I'm sorry," he said quietly. "It must be hard."

"I don't know why it still gets to me. I should be used to it by now." She felt the movement of his lips against her neck and in the window she saw the reflection of their faces so close together. She felt the warmth of his body against her back. She closed her eyes, feeling tense with the effort not to cry, to give in to the comfort of his embrace. Why did it still upset her so much? Why couldn't she just accept her parents for what they were and just forget it? But how could she forget the pain of so many years? Her throat ached and she felt the tears escape between her lashes.

He turned her around and kissed her forehead, her eyes. "You're crying."

"No, I'm not." Her voice was thick with tears.

"Go ahead and cry. I can take it."

"I'm not crying." Her body was rigid and tears ran down her face. "I'm not going to cry over this. I haven't cried for years and I'm not going to start now." She wiped at her eyes with her hand.

He handed her his handkerchief and his mouth quirked in a smile. "Stubborn, aren't you?"

"And stupid." She wiped her eyes and blew her nose. "I'm sorry I got so sappy. I don't know what got over me."

He led her back to the couch and drew her against him. "You look sad. And you're all tensed up." He began to stroke her hair, her back, in long, slow movements and she closed her eyes, wanting nothing more than to give herself over to his soothing touch and to relax in his arms.

"How's that?" he whispered.

"It feels good." He felt warm and comfortable and solid and she knew what she wanted more than anything was for him to kiss her. But her face was hidden against his chest. The thudding of his heart was noticeable against her cheek.

"Your hair smells nice," he said, burying his face in it, kissing her head.

She lifted her face and he relaxed his hold on her and smiled into her eyes, then bent down to kiss her forehead, her nose, her cheek with soft feathery touches. She moved restlessly against him, willing him to take her mouth, but he did not. He took his time, tantalizing her. He ran the tip of his tongue around the edge of her ear, along her jaw and up to the corner of her mouth, then turned back.

She slid her hands over his chest up to his shoulders. "Kiss me," she murmured, her body trembling with her need for him. "Please..."

He laid his hands against the sides of her face and looked into her eyes.

"You'd better know what you're asking," he warned, his voice husky.

"I'm asking for a kiss," she whispered. "One little kiss," she amended lightly, smiling at him, not wanting to give away the stormy feelings charging through her.

The thumb of his right hand caressed her bottom lip and his eyes narrowed slightly. "One little kiss," he agreed in a low voice. He lowered his head and touched his mouth to hers with gentle pressure. Her lips parted with a small sigh and she closed her eyes, savoring the moment, the taste, the scent, the feel of him. Silky, silvery sensations shivered through her.

His hands slid away from her face, moving around her to hold her closer, and the kiss grew deeper and more intimate until it was not a little kiss anymore, but something infinitely more passionate, infinitely more meaningful.

They opened their eyes at the same time, their lips still clinging. Slowly, carefully, he put her away from him.

"I'd better go home," he said quietly, coming to his feet.

No! she cried out silently, but the words did not form in her mouth. She watched him numbly as he left the room, sat motionless as she heard the back door open and close.

One little kiss. It was what she had asked for, yet she had got more than that, much more.

He could not get her out of his mind. Whatever he did, wherever he went, he could see her face in his mind's eye, the blue eyes that gave all her emotions away. But it wasn't only her face and eyes he enjoyed looking at, he admitted to himself as he lay in his sleeping bag that night. He liked seeing the small, neat shape of her in her faded jeans and T-shirt, the soft bounce of her breasts as she walked with that light, springy step of hers.

He admired her strength and determination, but she lacked the hard, sophisticated cynicism he had noticed in so many women in the past few years. There was something sweet and funny about her that attracted him, a certain vulnerability, too. He wasn't fooled for a moment by the lighthearted mockery and self-derision when she talked about herself. It hid a wealth of hurt and rejection. Through the open window he stared up at stars in the night sky, remembering the previous night.

He had wanted to make love to her, hold her, make her feel cared for and loved. He had wanted to touch and feel her soft, rounded curves, run his hands over her smooth skin. He pressed his eyes shut. God, he hadn't wanted a woman the way he wanted her for a long, long time.

And then something had happened. Something had stopped him. He closed his eyes and the pain rushed back hot and fierce, and it was not Jennifer he saw now behind his closed lids, but the dark, smiling eyes of another woman.

Jenny only saw him briefly the following week—a hasty cup of coffee, a hamburger out. Something was missing, she wasn't sure what. Mostly he seemed to avoid her, or try to. He didn't touch her or kiss her and at night she lay awake wondering if something was wrong.

Friday night he came to see her after work, a red rosebud in his hand.

"For you," he said, presenting it to her with a half smile. "Found it in the wilderness."

For a moment she was at a loss for words. A rose. He'd brought her a rose. It was a deep, rich red, fragrant perfection. She gazed at it, then back at Kane, who was watching her closely. She felt oddly breathless and warmth suffused her.

"Thank you. It's beautiful." She found a small, crystal bud vase that had belonged to her grandmother, filled it with water and gently put the rose in. She set it on the table and sat down.

"I love flowers," she said.

Kane straddled a chair. "They feed the soul, according to Mohammed."

"Mohammed?" She looked at him in surprise.

"I came across a quotation of his yesterday. I cut it out to show you." He fished a piece of newspaper out of his pocket and flattened it on his knee.

"If a man finds himself with bread in both hands," he read, *"he should exchange one loaf for some flowers: since the bread feeds the body indeed, but the flower feeds the soul."*

Jenny smiled. "That's beautiful." She reached out to the paper. "Can I see it?"

"You can have it."

She read the words again to herself. "I really like that," she said, looking up. "And it's true, you know."

He nodded. "I know. I've been so many places, but I always like it best when I'm in the country, in the mountains and fields where I can see things growing. It's very calming. A big reason for buying this house was the land around it. I want the garden to be peaceful and beautiful. I'm looking forward to it already."

"Yes." Her spirits sank. She came to her feet. "Would you like some coffee?"

"Please."

She was aware of him watching her as she busied herself at the counter, feeling the disappointment fill her again. Why did he have to mention his wretched garden now?

"I called Greenscape and Melton's," he announced as she spooned coffee into the mugs.

"I see." She tried to sound casual. All this week she'd thought about asking him if the landscaping people had come to look at the property yet, but pride had prevented her.

"I told them I didn't need their bids anymore and that I'd found somebody else."

Jenny frowned. "Who?" She glanced at him briefly before picking up the kettle to pour water into the mugs.

"You. I want you to landscape the garden for me."

Her hand stopped moving in midair, then in slow motion she put the kettle back down. Something was going on and she didn't understand. It didn't make sense. Why would he have changed his mind?

She swallowed hard and suddenly she understood. Anger and humiliation rose hot inside her.

"No, thank you," she said with as much dignity as she could muster.

Surprise flared in his eyes. "What do you mean, no? You wanted to do it! You told me how much it meant to you and now you're turning down the job?" He stood up abruptly, the chair scraping over the floor. "What's going on, Jennifer?"

She felt cold, icy cold. "What's going on? That's what I'd like to know. I don't need your charity, Kane. And I most certainly don't want your pity!"

"Pity?" The word rang in the silence and then comprehension dawned in his eyes. "Because of last Saturday night? Because of what you told me?"

"I'm not stupid, Kane. You've been acting strange all week and don't deny it."

He turned away from her, running his fingers through his hair. He looked up at the ceiling. "Jennifer," he said in a tightly controlled voice, "you've got it all wrong. I do not feel sorry for you." He turned back to her, anger radiating from his eyes. "And as for charity, let me say this: as a businessman I try not to take foolish risks. Calculated risks, yes, but not foolish ones. If I didn't have confidence in your capabilities, nothing would have persuaded me to offer you the job. It wouldn't make any sense."

She gripped the counter with both hands to steady herself and looked at him coldly. "Well, it still doesn't make any sense to me. A few weeks ago you called both those companies in Syracuse for an estimate. Now you suddenly change your mind. It makes me wonder, you know. I've got my pride. I don't want handouts. So you tell me, what made you change your mind?"

His pause was intentional. "I saw the Johnsons' yard," he said slowly, looking straight into her eyes. "And the McCormicks' flower garden. And the play park around the nursery school."

Her tongue refused to move, and in the silence he strode to the door, opened it and was gone.

Chapter Five

She sank down on a chair, feeling sick with regret and humiliation. She stared at the red rose and tears came into her eyes. How could she have misread him so? Were her feelings so wrapped up in her own pride that everything she saw was colored by it? How could she have been so unutterably stupid?

He had gone to see the work she had done before, the Johnsons' and McCormicks' yards, the play park... She hadn't known. And he must have liked what he saw or else he wouldn't have offered her the job. It wasn't his style at all, she should have known that. She closed her eyes and pressed her palms against the lids, hard. A kaleidoscope of burning colors swirled before her eyes and she released the pressure quickly.

She slept badly, surfacing eventually feeling as if she'd spent the night in a drafty jail cell. She groaned as she saw herself in the mirror. "I look like a dirty floor mop," she muttered in disgust.

It was Saturday, her busiest day. People were out working in their yards, getting ready to plant flowers and vegetables, and a constant trickle of customers stopped by the nursery to buy seedlings, seeds and other gardening supplies. Yet while her mouth was busy talking and smiling and giving advice, her mind kept playing back the past night's scene. She'd have to go to him and apologize. There was nothing else to do. Her stomach crawled at the thought of facing him.

At lunchtime Billy James stopped by. He wore faded jeans and an old sweatshirt and he needed a haircut.

"I wondered if you wanted to go and see a movie tonight," he asked.

"Thanks, Billy, but I can't. I've got other things to do." She dreaded these invitations. He meant well. He helped her out at times when something broke down that she couldn't fix herself. He never charged her for labor. Yet she didn't want to encourage him.

He sighed. "You're always busy." He looked sad and lonely and she felt sorry for him. He was having a hard time, she knew. Several months ago his wife had run off with an aging hippie with a graying beard, a braid down his back and a flowered van.

He glanced around, as if searching for something to say or do. "How's the pipe holding out?"

A couple of months ago one of the rain pipes had developed a bad leak and he had fixed it for her.

"No more problems. When are you going to send me a bill?"

He waved his hand. "Forget it."

"I'd like to pay you, Billy."

"You always do. The geraniums last year were real nice."

She'd placed two tubs full of bright red geraniums next to his shop entrance last summer after he'd refused payment for another job.

"I'll get you some more."

"Thanks. Well, I gotta go. See you around." He sauntered off to his Bronco and Jenny went back to work.

"Jenny!"

She turned, seeing Mary standing by the greenhouse with little Justin hanging on her bony hip like a sack of potatoes. The ability of some babies to fall asleep any place in any position was truly amazing.

Jenny jogged over to the greenhouse. "Hi. How's everything?"

"Fine, just fine. You wouldn't believe this, but I did it, I really did it." Mary looked very pleased with herself.

"You did what?" Jenny asked. "Tell off your mother-in-law? Eat snails?"

Mary grinned. "Something infinitely more courageous than that. I cleared a space for a vegetable garden. I'm going to give it a try." Her eyes sparked with the zeal of the newly converted.

Jenny looked grave. "You deserve a medal, but I hope you know what you're doing."

Mary's eyebrows shot up. "You told me it was easy!"

Jenny laughed out loud. "Gotcha! Come on in and we'll pick out some plants and seed. And do what I say! Okay?"

"Oh, don't worry, I will." Having grown up in a city apartment in Detroit, Mary was intimidated by anything green and alive. "My mother couldn't even keep geraniums alive on the balcony," she'd said once. "Pollution probably."

She'd had a hard time adjusting to the quiet, almost rural life of Guilford. She'd played basketball in college, and out of sheer boredom she'd started a women's basketball club in Guilford that played twice a week at the high school gym.

"So how's Kane?" Mary asked. "He must be the Hunk of the Year, at least in Guilford."

"His nose is too big," Jenny said evasively.

"I liked his nose."

"So did Justin. He wanted it for himself."

Mary laughed and Jenny opened the greenhouse door and stepped inside. She wasn't quite ready to discuss Kane. She prayed silently that he would accept her apologies tonight. The thought alone made her stomach churn with anxiety.

When Jenny drove up the circular driveway a little after seven that evening, Kane's car was gone. She sighed with disappointment and leaned on the steering wheel. She'd showered, washed her hair and put on clean white slacks and a sky blue shirt. She'd picked an armful of daffodils as a peace offering. All this effort for nothing. She climbed out of the pickup truck and tried the front door. It was locked. It would have to be, of course, with all the tools and equipment lying around all over the house. Maybe he had just gone out to get something to eat.

She lowered herself onto the steps, carefully putting down the large glass fishbowl that held the daffodils. She put her elbows on her knees and rested her chin in her hands. She could wait for a while. It was quiet and peaceful here, the twittering and chirping of the birds in the greenery the only sounds in the silence.

Half an hour later she was about to give up her vigil when she heard a car come up the driveway. The gray Continental came into view and stopped in front of her pickup. Kane climbed out, tall and lean, coming toward her with long, easy strides. Her nerves began to jump.

"Hello, Jennifer." He carried a Styrofoam cup with a lid. Coffee, probably. His face was impassive and she couldn't tell a thing from his expression.

"Hi." Hastily she picked up the flowers and came to her feet. Kane fished a key from his jeans pocket and opened the door.

"You want to come in?"

"Please. I want to talk to you. I waited because I thought you might just be out to get something to eat."

"I was."

She walked ahead of him into the hall and turned to face him. "Kane...I came to apologize," she said nervously. "I'm really sorry about what I said. I'm sorry I misunderstood your motives. I was a real jerk."

He shrugged. "Forget it."

She shook her head. "Kane..."

"It's all right, Jennifer," he said impatiently.

"No, it isn't. It wasn't. I mean, you had every right to be angry with me."

"I was, but I'll live."

She followed him as he climbed up the stairs, her heart heavy. He was still angry. She looked at his back, his long legs as they moved easily up the stairs. Their footsteps sounded loud and hollow on the bare wood. It was almost spooky, this empty old house without a stick of furniture in it. He led her to the small room where he still slept on the floor. A storm lamp stood on the floor along with a candle stuck on a jar lid.

She held out the daffodils. "I brought you a peace offering, something to cheer up your room." She looked around, then set the flowers down on the floor in a patch of evening sunlight that sneaked through the window. She stepped back to examine the effect. They were like a burst of golden light, cheering the room.

"Thank you," Kane said levelly.

She felt a hot surge of temper. "Listen! I came here to apologize." Her voice shook. "You tell me it's all right, but it isn't! You're still mad at me! The least you can do is to mean it when you say it's all right! I apologized. What else can I do?"

He tossed his cap on top of a pile of papers and heaved a sigh. "I'm sorry," he said. "I'm not in a very good mood. It's been one hassle after another with this house the whole damned day." He rubbed his chin wearily. There were lines of fatigue around his mouth and his eyes looked dull. She felt a softening inside her. She wanted to put her arms around him and smooth out the lines on his face.

Instead she moved to the door. "I'll leave you alone then."

"Please, don't go, Jennifer."

They gazed at each other for a long moment.

"I'm sorry," he said again, glancing over at the daffodils. "And thank you for the flowers. They're beautiful. Did you grow them?"

"My grandfather planted them, years ago. There's a big patch of them in back of the house and every spring there are more." She looked at them uncertainly, not knowing what else to say or do.

"Sit down," he offered, gesturing at the sleeping bag.

She sat down cross-legged and he lowered himself next to her, pulling up his knees. He began to pry loose the plastic lid on the coffee cup. "Want some?" He held the cup out to her. "Black, no sugar."

She hesitated. "It's yours."

"I'll be glad to share," he said on a quasi-formal note that made her smile. The tension in her stomach eased.

She took the cup and had a careful sip, aware of a sense of intimacy in sharing the coffee, drinking from the same cup. Through the open window the cool evening breeze wafted in, carrying in sweet spring scents.

"Where did you go to eat?" she asked for something to say.

"Sammy's Superduper Diner. Where else? I had a steak. It was awful. Give me rice and lentils any time." A smile played around his mouth.

"Why do you stay here? Why not sleep at the motel?"

He gave a crooked little grin. "This appeals to my sense of the absurd."

"It must." She handed him back the cup and watched him take a swallow of the weak brew. She wondered if his nose ever got in the way, which was a dumb thought. It certainly didn't get in the way when he kissed her, which he hadn't done in ages.

He lowered his cup. "You're staring."

"I was looking at your nose." She wondered if he had any hang-ups about it. "I like your nose."

He ran his finger over the hump. "I'm quite attached to it."

"That's terrible," she came back.

He grinned. "I know, but I couldn't resist. My nose has been the subject of many jokes. My friends used to call me Drommie. Here, have some more coffee."

"Drommie?"

"From dromedary. My older sister, Casey, started it by calling me Dromedary Nose, but that got too long. I'd be playing ball in the street and she'd come out to call me in for dinner. She'd yell, 'Hey Drommie! Dinner's ready!' She only needed to do it once for every kid on the block to pick up on it."

Jenny laughed. "Did you mind?"

"Mind? Heck, no. I like my nose. My younger sister keeps asking me when I'm having it fixed. She'd be shocked if I actually did, though."

She longed to touch his nose, his face, his mouth. She wanted to taste his kisses, run her fingers through his hair. The cup suddenly trembled in her hand and she brought it carefully to her mouth and sipped the coffee. It was much too intimate sitting so close to him in the small, empty room with its curtainless windows.

"I've been thinking," he said conversationally. "If you really wanted to study landscape architecture, you could do it. There are scholarships and maybe your parents could help."

She handed him back the cup, feeling suddenly uneasy. "Sure. But you're forgetting one thing, Kane. I don't really want to go back to college."

"Why not?"

"I told you before. I'd rather be here doing what I'm doing. I'm happy here."

"And waste your talent?"

She laughed. "You're being very dramatic and I doubt it very much, Kane."

He finished the last of the coffee and put the empty cup on the floor, his eyes not leaving her face. "I saw the different places you landscaped. You have the eye of an artist. That's why you put those daffodils right there in that patch of light. If you love landscaping so much, then you're wasting your talents and efforts sitting here in this nursery."

She smiled blithely. "Oh, but I'm happy while I'm wasting. That should count for something." She moved, trying to get to her feet, but his hand clamped on her arm.

"You want to run away?" he asked softly.

"From what?"

"From the truth. You can't do that, you know. The truth has this nasty habit of following like a shadow."

"I do like it when you get philosophical."

"Shut up," he said softly, giving her wrist a forceful yank and pulling her back down next to him. "What's the matter, Jennifer?"

"Nothing's the matter. I haven't a clue what you're talking about."

"Sure you do. You don't like talking about your future. You don't like talking about your family, because they're all so ambitious and apparently had higher expectations for you and—"

"Why don't you mind your own business, Kane?" she said cheerfully, feeling like she wanted to beat him over the head with any handy object. "Give it up. I'm not interested."

He gave her a dark look. "I've seen the work you have done," he went on, ignoring her words. "It's not the work of an amateur. You know what you're doing. You have a feel for color and shape and texture. You have talent, and you're not doing much with it."

Her body tensed. She took a deep breath and looked right into his eyes. "You have no right, no right to criticize me, Kane."

"I'm not criticizing you, Jennifer," he said quietly. He took her hand. "I care about you, about your work and your talent. I admire the work you've done, but I don't understand you."

I admire the work you've done. It was pure delight to hear those words! She smiled at him. "You'll get to understand me. Just give it time."

He smiled back, a crooked little smile as if he wasn't quite sure he would. There was a stillness in the room and she wanted to reach out to him, put her arms around him, but something held her back. For a long moment they stared at each other. Then, with a sigh, she looked away. Darkness was creeping into the room and through the window she saw the sky streaked in delicate pastel shades.

She heard him strike a match and light the candle. Soft light spread through the room.

"When are you going to start on my place?" he asked evenly.

The tension flowed out of her. She straightened her back. "Tomorrow. Will you still be here?"

"I can be."

"I'll have to ask you some questions, and I'll need a property survey and..." She shrugged. "We'll talk about it tomorrow."

"You'll need to give me a cost estimate and a contract."

"Of course." She came slowly to her feet, tucking her hair behind her ears. "I'll be off now. I'll see you in the morning."

He grasped her hand and pulled her back down. "What's your hurry?" He draped his arm around her shoulder. "We didn't really make up properly, did we?" There were laughing lights in his eyes and she could feel her face grow warm under his teasing gaze.

"I have no idea what you're talking about."

"Miss Innocent." He lowered his face toward her until his nose touched hers. "I want to kiss you," he whispered. "Do you want to kiss me?"

"I'll have to think about it." Her heart was racing, her body aglow with magic feeling. She wanted to kiss him, hold him, touch him.

He laughed softly. "Okay, you think about it while I keep my hands busy." He caressed her breasts, very gently. "Take your time."

The touch of his hands sent her senses soaring. She slipped her arms around his neck. "I thought about it."

"You want to kiss me?"

"Yes."

"Okay, let's do it. Who first?"

She began to laugh. "Kane! You're a horrible tease."

"It's so much fun to tease you." He nibbled her ear and she squirmed in his arms.

"Kane!" she muttered, and then his mouth found hers and suddenly all the teasing was gone and there was just their mouths and hands and the overwhelming feeling of need and longing.

They broke away at the same time. Jenny leaned against the wall and closed her eyes. Her heart was racing at an alarming speed and it was hard to breathe.

For a few moments it was very quiet in the room, then she looked sideways, finding Kane looking at her, his eyes dark and stormy. She swallowed hard and came to her feet.

"I have to go now."

He stood up, too. "Jennifer?" He took her hand and looked into her eyes.

"What?" Her voice sounded oddly husky.

"No games, all right?"

She shook her head. "No."

It was a promise, she realized, and the thought of it warmed and excited her.

He walked with her down the stairs, holding the candle to light the steps. Dark shadows danced wildly along the walls as they moved down. Like some Gothic novel, she thought, grinning to herself.

Kane opened the pickup door for her, closing it after she'd climbed in. He leaned forward through the open window, his face very close to hers. Then he kissed her firmly, withdrawing almost instantly. With trembling fingers she inserted the key into the ignition and turned it. Kane stepped back from the car.

"I'll see you in the morning."

She nodded without answering, revved the engine and raced down the driveway to the road.

He wanted her. He had wanted to make love to her in that bare little room upstairs. Yet he had not tried to keep her with him. Something was holding him back.

She didn't know if she was relieved or frightened.

Kane lay on top of his sleeping bag and stared at the daffodils. No woman had ever given him flowers. No woman in the last few years had made him feel the way Jennifer made him feel.

No games. He wanted no games, but what was it that he did want?

One thing he had wanted was to make love to her, here, on his sleeping bag, like he had wanted to make love to her last Saturday night. But that wasn't all he wanted. That alone wasn't enough.

He closed his eyes and groaned.

Something was happening inside him. He felt overwhelmed by his overpowering need for her, not just the physical, but his need for closeness and intimacy on an emotional level. But fear was taking over, fear of getting in too deep, of taking chances. His contradictory feelings confused him. He wanted her. He wanted to get closer, get to know her better. He needed a sense of belonging, of intimacy, yet it scared him to try. What if it didn't work? He wasn't sure he was ready for the loss and the failure. He wasn't sure if he had the guts for another commitment.

He kept thinking of Anne, of their life together, of all the loving and laughter, of the terrible pain when they'd lost Kevin, of the aching loneliness when he lost her, too.

To start all over was terrifying.

It was just after nine Sunday morning when Jenny drove up to the house again. The front door was open so she let herself in, calling for Kane as she entered, but no answer came. Was he still asleep? No, she decided, not with the front door open. She walked through the house, and finally saw him on the back porch, sitting on the steps.

She tapped the grimy window. "Kane?"

He looked up, grinned, and waved at her to come outside.

"Good morning," he greeted her as she stepped out onto the porch. The boards creaked ominously under her weight.

"Hi. Boy, it is glorious!"

"And I make you work."

"What better work than this on a day like this? Can't think of anything I'd rather do."

"Good, then I won't have to feel guilty."

"Not for a minute. I brought some breakfast," she announced, putting a box down on the weathered boards of the porch. "Is this place safe? It looks like it's going to collapse any minute now."

"It will hold up for another morning. So what have you got there?"

"Coffee and brown bread and cheese and honey sandwiches and boiled eggs and bananas."

"Honey sandwiches? Sounds good, but rather unorthodox."

"I'm not a very orthodox person, and I tried to think of things that were easy and wouldn't make a mess." She took out a small blue checkered tablecloth and spread it on the gray boards. He watched her, his face amused, as she set out the food and filled two mugs with coffee from a Thermos bottle.

"Thanks." He took one of the cups. "A perfect morning for a picnic breakfast."

She felt a thrill of joy. "It was fun to do. Eating by myself all the time is no great kick."

"I know what you mean." For a moment he stared at the green wilderness spread out before them, then shaking his head, he picked up an egg and began to peel it. The sun touched his hair, picking out the few silvery strands that streaked the black at his temples.

She felt a lump in her throat. She could always tell when the past intruded in his thoughts. She wanted to hold him and chase the sadness from his eyes, see the warm glints of humor return. Yet she sat quietly next to him, not touching, feeling sad and afraid. He had loved his wife. She wondered what Anne had been like, what she had looked like, what kind of person she'd been, what sort of relationship she and Kane had had.

A cool, fragrant breeze wafted across her face and arms and she took a slow, deep breath, closing her eyes and lifting her face to the sun.

"Tell me," Kane said after a moment, waving his hand around, "how do you go about a job like this? Where do you start?"

She put her coffee cup down. "First I need to see the property survey, so I know exactly where the boundaries are, and stake them out if necessary. We'll take soil samples of course, and look at the sun-shade situation, the different elevations and all that sort of thing. And let's not forget a budget. Then I'll draw up a plan, a design. You'll need to tell me what sort of garden you prefer and what kind of bushes and plants you like. A lot of what I'd do depends on your preferences and the kind of money you want to spend. You've seen the other places I've done. They're very different. Anyway, I'll come up with a preliminary design and a cost estimate before I do any pulling and digging."

He gave her a close look. "And who does the pulling and digging?"

"I could subcontract that to a company in Syracuse, but I'd rather use local labor. I know a lot of people here, and the equipment is available. The economic situation isn't too good around here and extra work is always appreciated. It's more cost-effective, too."

For a moment he studied her silently, a smile playing around his mouth. "Cost estimate, subcontract, cost-effective," he repeated. "Somehow I wasn't expecting that jargon from you."

She gave him her sweetest smile. "I like to fool people into thinking I know what I'm talking about. When you're a mere amateur you need all the help you can get."

His eyes narrowed as he scanned her face. "Why do I get the impression you're making fun of me?"

She looked at him wide-eyed. "I have no idea. Maybe because you were condescending?"

"I was?" He frowned. "I'm sorry, I didn't mean to be."

"Apology accepted."

"Thank you," he said gravely. He held out his cup. "Is there any more coffee?"

She poured them each another cup and leaned back against the railing, letting out a sigh of contentment as she surveyed the peaceful surroundings. She felt her skin soak up the sunshine, smelled the scents of moist soil and tender greenery.

She half closed her eyes and peeked at Kane through her lashes. He looked so good sitting there in the sun, his lower arms bare and brown, his long legs stretched out lazily on the boards. She wondered what it would be like to make love with him, to see his body without the covering of clothes.

She got up hastily, breaking her train of thought. "We'd better take a walk and have another look, okay? Oh, and I almost forgot. Do you have a floor plan of the house?"

"Of course. Why?"

"We have to think of the views when we draw up a design, so we'll need to know where the rooms and the windows are." She took her notebook and pencil and skipped down the few steps leading down from the porch. She couldn't wait to get started.

For a couple of hours they tramped through the wet, grassy grounds, talking and figuring and asking questions of each other.

"What about a pond? A fountain?" she asked. "This is a natural place for it. It's always wet. But I'll check it out first with someone who knows."

"A pond, fine, but no fountains. I want everything as natural as possible. And no cutesy trolls with wheelbarrows or windmills or plaster of paris statues."

Jenny laughed and let out a sigh of relief. "Good, I don't do statues." Adrenaline was gushing and she couldn't wait to get started.

Kane looked at her with amusement. "I like enthusiasm in a woman. Your face is glowing and you can barely stand still. You're sure you want to do this?"

She grinned at him, then arranged her face in an expression of indifference and shrugged. "Not really, but a girl needs to eat."

"Hah!" He stood very close, eyes laughing into hers, and for a heart-stopping moment she thought he was going to kiss her. But he just stood there and looked at her with a devilish glint in his eyes until she could stand it no longer. Her hand reached out and touched his cheek, then, standing on tiptoe, she kissed him. His mouth was warm and in-

viting and her pulse began to race frantically. She withdrew,
taking a step back.

"Why did you do that?" he asked, smiling.

"Because I wanted to."

"Do you always go around kissing people in gardens?"

She grinned. "Only the ones I like."

In the afternoon Kane left to go back to New York. She
worked for the rest of the day and well into the night, making several outlines of the area based on the measurements
from the survey report. She went back to the house and took
more measurements, making notes of the plants and trees
already there, drawing in the paths and trees on her sketch.
Kane was gone and the house was locked up. He'd said he'd
be back the next Saturday.

Back at home she studied the information, then set to
work roughing a design. All during the week as she watered
the seedlings in the greenhouse, her mind was busy with
Kane's garden. Ideas kept coming to her—from one came
another and she kept stopping in the middle of her work to
rush back to her office to look something up or make a
change in the design.

If her mind wasn't occupied with the garden, it was busy
thinking about Kane. At night she dreamed of him, sensuous and erotic dreams that left her restless and unsatis-
fied. She kept hearing his voice at the oddest times, saw his
face before her mind's eye, the big nose, the laughing brown
eyes, the confident stance of his body. She longed for his
touch, she longed to be in his arms again.

Saturday seemed years away.

It amazed him how easily she'd taken possession of his
mind and thoughts and dreams. He thought of her all the
time, seeing the soft mouth, the easy smile, the shine in her

blue eyes. Her enthusiasm for the job was infectious, and he was impressed by the measure of knowledge and professionalism she displayed.

Lost in thought, Kane stood in front of his window overlooking the bright lights of New York, then finally he turned away. He didn't bother to close the curtains. It wouldn't make the room look any warmer. Beautiful as it was, it was not a home and he was becoming increasingly aware of it. He'd much rather be with Jenny in her dinky little house. It had a warm, lived-in look despite the old furniture and worn carpeting and linoleum. She'd managed, somehow, to give the place some character, some sense of home.

He wanted a home again. A place to feel happy, a place to share with someone else. Jennifer. He felt good in her company. With her he felt an inner peace, as if her presence eased the stresses of his life.

He moved into the bedroom, his footsteps quiet on the soft cream carpeting. He stared at the big bed with a mingling of despair and frustration. Damn, he wanted her with him tonight, in his own bed. He wanted to make love to her, feel her warm, smooth skin against him.

Not too fast. Take it easy, take it slow. Don't be stupid and ruin it all.

Well, he would wait. For how long he didn't know. He stripped off his shirt and threw it across the room in frustration.

Chapter Six

I understand you're landscaping the grounds around the Cleever house." Jenny's father looked at her over the rim of his reading glasses, his heavy eyebrows above the penetrating gray eyes raised in question. His gray hair was thick and bushy and his general appearance was one of power and strength. In court he was magnificent. Jennifer felt sorry for the poor saps who came up against him. She almost felt sorry for herself, knowing what was coming.

"That's right."

"Why didn't you tell us about it?"

"I didn't?" She shrugged casually. "I must have forgotten to mention it."

There was a pregnant silence. "It's not the sort of thing you forget to mention, Jenny. It's a big job. There must be several acres around that old house. An impressive wilderness last time I saw it. Don't you think you're being just a little bit ambitious taking on that job?"

"Heavens, no, Dad," she said cheerfully. "Not a little bit. A whole lot."

He gave her a look of surprise, eyebrows rising even higher. "Why, then, did you accept it?"

"Because I wanted to." She smiled. "And because I'm good and I've got lots of talent." She challenged him with her eyes.

"How do you know you're good?"

"Hey, what is this, Dad? Am I in a court of law or in my parents' living room? Don't worry. I know what I'm doing." She gathered up the coffee cups and cake plates and stacked them on a tray.

"I just hope you're right. Getting stuck in the middle of a project like that would be embarrassing."

Her stomach clenched hard like a fist, but she managed to smile. "It would, wouldn't it?" She picked up the tray and left the room.

Her mother was in the kitchen clearing away the remnants of their dinner. She put several slices of roast beef in a shallow plastic container and poured gravy over them.

"Why don't you take this, Jenny? There's plenty left for us for tomorrow."

Jenny sighed inwardly. Why did her mother have to do this? Give her food every time she visited? As if she thought Jenny was starving herself. As if she thought Jenny didn't have enough money to feed herself. Her mother never gave anything to Suzanne, at least not that Jenny had noticed. Of course, Suzanne was making a pile of money and was probably eating out every other night anyway.

"Thanks." She put the tray on the counter and started loading the cups and saucers into the dishwasher. "Dad doesn't think I can do the Cleever house grounds. He thinks I'm being too ambitious."

"We don't want you to get in over your head, dear."

"Mom," she began quietly, trying hard to stay calm. "Don't you think I'm smart enough to figure that out for myself? Don't you think that at twenty-six I'm capable of making these decisions for myself?"

Her mother lifted her perfectly coiffed head and gave her an assessing look. "But you've never done anything of this size and you are not qualified. The problems involved—"

"I know the problems involved, Mom. I'm not stupid. And it would be nice... it would be nice if for once... for *once* you'd have just a little confidence in me." Her voice shook. She knew she had to leave before her anger made her say things she'd regret. She closed her eyes briefly, trying to calm herself. It frightened her how suddenly anger had risen to the surface.

She picked up her purse from the kitchen chair and walked to the door. "I'm going now. Thanks for dinner."

Why do I keep coming? she asked herself as she drove out of the driveway. Why do I keep putting myself through this? Because they're my parents, she answered herself. Because if you can't go home anymore, then too much is lost.

As the man closed the door behind him, Kane leaned back in his chair and grinned. He'd found his man! Twenty-three prescreened applicants he'd had to interview before he'd found the person he wanted. Greg Morrison, twenty-nine, ambitious, knowledgeable and well-traveled. On paper most of them had had similar qualifications, yet in the interviews they simply hadn't held up. But Greg Morrison— skinny, red-haired, freckled and funny—was his man. His knowledge of people, his sensitivity to cultural differences coupled with a humorous outlook on life had sold Kane.

Greg Morrison, Kane reflected, was going to make his life a lot easier. He would take over most of the routine traveling, leaving Kane to do the managing stateside. His desire to settle down, to stay closer to home, had only grown over the past couple of months.

Four years of loneliness were enough. Four years of travel and frantic working were enough. It was time to calm down, to start living again. Time to wake up in the morning with a woman in his bed. Time to love again and be happy.

He thought of the house and the furnishing of it, of the magnificent garden Jennifer would create. In his thoughts she already was part of it all. He wanted her in that house with him. He wanted to look at her across the table while he ate his meals. He wanted her in his bed. He wondered why she'd hidden herself in that small town for the past few years, bottling up all that sensuality and hiding her talent. It did not make sense to him. She could go far if she decided she wanted to try. Why didn't she even want to talk about it? Well, he wasn't going to let it lie. He picked up the phone and buzzed his secretary.

"Marian?"

"Yes? Oh, before I forget, I've got your tickets for Tokyo. Everything's in order."

"Thanks." He frowned in irritation. He hadn't counted on going to Japan on Monday. Three weeks, damn! It was a bad time to be away from the house. He hoped the builders knew what they were doing and didn't louse it up while he was away. They were supposed to be the best around, but he wasn't so sure.

Three weeks without seeing Jennifer. That was worse.

"Kane?"

"Yes?"

"Is there anything else?"

He rubbed his chin and sighed. "Oh, yes. Find out what university has a degree program in landscape architecture."

"Where? Here?"

"In New York State."

The answer came ten minutes later. "City College has a bachelor's program in urban landscape architecture and SUNY in Syracuse has both a bachelor's and a master's program and a more elaborate curriculum."

"Syracuse it is. Get me their catalog, prospectus, whatever, okay?"

There was a short silence. "Sure. Are you going back to school?"

He laughed. "I just might. Once this Greg Morrison takes over I'm going to have time on my hands."

Too bad Greg couldn't start earlier. The summer was still going to be hell to get through. There were trips scheduled to East Africa and South America. He wouldn't see much of Jennifer. And on Monday he was going to Japan for three weeks. But once fall came, he'd have time.

He couldn't wait.

"Close your eyes and open your mouth." Jenny looked down at Kane's face. He lay stretched out in the grass in blissful relaxation.

Obediently Kane closed his eyes and opened his mouth. Jenny slowly lowered a big red strawberry onto his tongue.

"Eat it."

He did.

"Now you have to admit," she said, "this is the juiciest, sweetest strawberry you have ever tasted in your entire life."

"Not a doubt about it."

"Old Jim tells everybody I grow the biggest, sweetest strawberries in all of New York State."

"I wouldn't want to argue with him. I had a discussion with him the other day. When he starts talking, he won't quit. I couldn't get away to save my life."

Jenny laughed. "That's why he likes the job. He gets to talk to all the customers. I think he's lonely."

She offered him another strawberry which he caught between his pursed lips. Eyes still closed he slowly ate the berry. "Not as sweet as you, though," he murmured.

"Flatterer." She put a berry in her own mouth.

In one smooth movement he sat up and pulled her face toward him. "And you're driving me crazy, you know that?"

"No," she whispered against his lips.

"Yes, you are." He kissed her deeply, hungrily. His hand slipped to the front of her shirt and slowly began to unbutton it. "You have too many things on," he whispered. "I want to see you, touch you." He slid the shirt over her shoulders and down her arms, all in slow-motion, kissing her as he went along. He unhooked her bra in the back and dropped it on top of the shirt in the grass. He cupped her breasts, one in each hand, and bent his head down to kiss first one, then the other. A wild, painful hunger took possession of her body, her mind.

"You're beautiful," he said softly, raising his face to hers, smiling crookedly as he noticed the heat rushing through her, flushing her face. With one finger he began to trace circles around her breast while his other hand quickly removed his own shirt. His chest was very brown and lightly matted with dark hair and her heart raced as she looked at him. He gathered her to him and her breasts pressed against his chest.

She wanted this to happen—she wanted to let go and be swept away by the sweet desire that made her body tremble and glow. Never before had she experienced such deep, intense longing for a man. Reaching up, she laced her fingers through the thick, dark hair, drawing his face toward her.

She searched for his mouth, found it open and eager, and their tongues touched in moist invitation.

He drew back with a groan, taking in a deep, uneven breath. For an endless moment he looked into her eyes, then he reached over to pick up her shirt and draped it over her shoulders.

"What's wrong?" she whispered.

He closed his eyes briefly. "Nothing, nothing." He reached out and drew her hard against him.

She wanted to make love. She wanted to make love with him more than anything in the world, here behind the rose-bushes in the warm sunshine. Yet he had withdrawn from her again. She felt an aching disappointment, mingled with a sudden fear. Was he thinking of his wife when she was in his arms? Was it still his wife he really wanted?

She wanted to ask, but couldn't find the courage to utter the words. She straightened away from him, wanting suddenly to be free of his embrace.

"I'm sorry," he muttered, releasing her. "I didn't mean to get so carried away." He raked his hand through his hair and peered up into the sky, following the path of an airplane humming high above. "I'm leaving for Japan early tomorrow morning."

"I didn't know." She began to button her shirt.

"I didn't know myself. I'll be gone three weeks. It came up unexpectedly."

She was silent, trying to digest the news, trying not to feel disappointment. She hugged her knees to her chest and watched a bee buzz around the roses—big yellow blooms with a sweet, delicate perfume that hung in the warm summer air. She didn't want Kane to go, but it would always be that way. Traveling was part of his job. Absentmindedly she pulled out a blade of grass, then threw it away.

"What are you thinking?" he asked.

"Japan is far away." Her voice sounded oddly husky and she cleared her throat, looking away.

"What else?"

"Never mind."

"Don't *never mind* me. I want to know what you're thinking."

"Did you travel a lot when you were married?"

He gave her a searching look. "Quite a bit. Not as much as the last few years, though."

"Did your wife mind?"

"She understood. She was a very busy career woman herself. But it wasn't easy." He sighed. "I wish I didn't have to go, Jennifer, but there's nothing I can do about it. It will get easier once the summer is over. I've just hired someone who can take over most of the traveling. He'll start work in September. I should have done it earlier, but I didn't care about being gone all the time. There was nothing for me here, so I just got on the planes and did what needed to be done." His eyes held hers. "But things have changed. All I want now is to be with you." He draped one arm around her shoulders and drew her back against him. "I'm so tired of all those solitary meals and that empty apartment. All I can think of is being with you, talking with you, watching you."

She felt a softness invade her, a stirring of love and sweetness. Maybe she was worried for nothing, seeing problems where there were none. She closed her eyes and relaxed against him, smelling the familiar scent of his sun-warmed skin. The hair on his bare chest tickled her cheek.

His hands played with her hair, winding strands of it around his fingers. "After I get back I'd like you to come to the city and I'll cook you the best pepper steak you've ever had. I still owe you that pepper steak."

"You owe me nothing."

He lifted her face to his. "I owe you more than you know."

"Like what?"

"You make me feel good. You make me feel there's some sense in my life again."

Her heart ached with love. "You make me feel good, too," she said huskily. "I'll miss you."

"I'll miss you, too."

Several days later a box arrived in the mail with a note from Suzanne.

Mom told me there's a man in your life, the new owner of the Cleever house, no less. Well, it was about time you found yourself someone again, kiddo, but be careful with those big city boys! You have no idea how they can fool you. Make sure he isn't married. Anyway, so much for the advice. I was thinking that with a man like him (Mom told me he's some sort of hotshot art dealer) you'd probably need more than jeans and T-shirts. I was going through my closet the other day and I thought I'd send you some of the things I don't wear anymore. I didn't even know I had half of this stuff. Keep anything you like and give the rest away. Have fun! Love, Suzanne.

For three days Jenny glared at the box without opening it, pride fighting with her curiosity. She should send the damned clothes back without opening the box. *Be careful with those big city boys.* What did Suzanne think she was? Some nitwit teenager without a lick of sense? She sighed wearily. Why were they all treating her like a child? Her mother with her food, and now Suzanne with these clothes...as if she were a poor relative. Jenny gave a dry laugh. Well, she *was* a poor relative. She gave the box a kick and went outside.

Having kicked the box a few times more, her pride lost and her curiosity won. What the hell? She might as well see what was inside it. "When you are poor," she muttered to herself, "pride is an expensive luxury."

There were several dresses, a couple of skirts, silky blouses and even two pairs of almost new shoes. The labels were, of course, impressive, as was to be expected from her sister. Jenny stared at the clothes spread out on the big brass bed. How could Suzanne not want these things anymore? There was nothing wrong with them. They weren't even out of fashion. She lifted up one of the dresses, a simple silk affair in a delicate amethyst color. It was gorgeous. She held it in front of her and looked in the mirror. The color looked beautiful, giving her eyes a silvery shine she'd never seen before.

She peeled off her jeans and shirt and slipped the dress over her head. She fastened the tiny round, covered buttons, holding her breath, staring at the mirror. It was perfect. It couldn't have fit her better. She exhaled slowly, taking in the shimmery, silky reflection of herself. Perfect. Perfect for New York. She smiled at herself. What would Kane think? She slid her hands along her hips, the fabric soft and sensuous against her fingertips. It was a good feeling wearing something so feminine.

She'd had beautiful clothes herself as a child and in college when her father was still footing the bill for her expenses. But once on her own, working in the nursery, she'd had to make do with her own meager income and clothes had been scratched from her budget. She hadn't minded. Jeans were comfortable, and she had had enough nice clothes in her closet to last her a while. But now, after several years, they were outdated and looked wrong.

She turned and examined her other side in the mirror. It really was a gorgeous dress. Maybe she should have her hair styled. Have it cut shorter, as her mother had suggested. She noticed herself frown in the mirror. No, she'd leave it the way it was.

That evening she wrote a short thank-you note to her sister before sitting down to do some paperwork.

The following weeks seemed endless, and when Kane's call finally came after he'd returned, her heart made a leap of joy at the sound of his voice over the telephone.

"How have you been?" he asked.

"Fine," she squeaked. She took a deep breath. "The clearing is finished and I've started planting some of the shrubs. Your inspection is welcome any time, sir."

He laughed. She loved the sound of it. She pressed the phone closer to her ear as if it would make him closer, too.

"I can't wait to see it, but first I want you to come into the city for some dining, dancing and debauchery. Not necessarily in that order."

"Sounds good to me." Real good, she added to herself, feeling a delicious stir of anticipation. "How was Japan?"

"Fascinating, as always. I'll tell you all about it. What would you like to do Friday night? A concert? A play? After the pepper steak, that is."

Nothing, she answered silently. *All I want to do is be with you—anywhere.* "I'm easy. I'll leave it up to you."

"Mmm . . . I'll see what I can do. What time are you coming in?"

She gave him the details of her arrival and he told her he'd be there to pick her up. "I can't wait to see you again," he said, his voice low and husky. "I keep having the most disturbing dreams."

"Me too," she whispered.

There was a silence. "I suppose I should say something appropriate and hang up now," he said, and she could hear the smile in his voice. "I wonder why I'm hanging on."

"Would you like me to say something appropriate and hang up?"

"No. Just go on talking. I like your voice. Have I told you that?"

"No, and you're just saying that."

"That's not a very gracious way to react to a compliment. And I wasn't just saying that. I noticed your voice the first time I met you."

"Nobody has ever commented on my voice before."

"Beauty is in the ear of the beholder."

Jenny laughed. "Okay, you win. I'm pleased you like my voice."

"Good. And it's not all I like, either, but I'll save that for when I see you."

"Tell me now. I need to hear it."

He chuckled. "It would be highly inappropriate, not to speak of the inconvenience of wires melting."

She laughed. "I'll wait then." There was another silence. Jenny could think of a number of things to say, but none of them were appropriate, either. The silence echoed between them.

"Jennifer, I think we'd better hang up now."

"I guess so."

"Good night, then. I'll see you on Friday."

"Good night, Kane." She waited to hear the click on the other end before lowering the receiver. Minutes later she still stood there, smiling at the wall like a fool.

Despite the masses of milling people in the station, she found Kane easily. Internal radar, no doubt. She rushed into his arms and held him tight. He kissed her briefly, quickly, but his eyes promised more later, away from the madding crowd.

He looked as wonderful as ever. She was never disappointed. The same dancing eyes, the same tempting mouth, the same strong, sensitive hands.

Once inside the apartment, she didn't stop to even look around. She was in his arms, hugging him hard, pressing her cheek against the solid warmth of his neck. "I missed you," she muttered, then lifted her face to search for his mouth. She drowned in his kiss, a mingling of breath and life, an impatient, restless searching, a dance of tongues touching and withdrawing. A soft moan rose in her throat.

"You're magic," he murmured, his mouth leaving hers to drop soft kisses all over her face. "You do terrifying things to my heart. You make me crazy."

"Good," she whispered, stroking his chest, feeling the beat of his heart under her palm.

He drew back, taking a ragged breath, then giving her a roguish smile. "Welcome to my castle." His hands slid down her sides and came to rest on her hips. "Let me show you around."

The apartment was vast and beautifully decorated, very chic, very tasteful. He showed her the rooms, talking about the art he had collected from around the world. Jenny looked and listened. It was a showplace without any real warmth or personality. Did he really live here? she wondered. It seemed strange to think he, a man of such warmth and love, spent his time in this cold place, eating, sleeping, working. There was no sign of the presence of a woman. Nothing to indicate that at some time a woman—or a child—had lived in these rooms.

Until she entered his study and noticed the photograph on his desk. Her heart lurched at the sight of it and she felt a sick feeling in the pit of her stomach. Anne was dark-haired, beautiful, smiling. The small boy's face was serious with dark eyes and curly hair. A beautiful child. She couldn't help but stare at the photograph until she felt Kane's hand grip her fingers.

She glanced at him quickly and swallowed hard. "Your wife and son?" she asked unnecessarily.

He nodded. "Anne and Kevin."

"Do you think of them often?"

"Not as often as I used to, and it doesn't hurt as much anymore. I think . . . I think I've come to terms with the inevitable." He held her eyes. "They are part of my past. The most important part," he said slowly. "But I need someone for my present and my future." The question was in his eyes and the blood began to pound in her ears. The grip on her fingers intensified and he drew her to him, slipping his arms around her.

"Please think about it," he said quietly.

She looked into his eyes, seeing the dark glitter there, and the warmth that filled her grew deeper and more intense. For a moment they looked silently at each other, and the room filled with fragile emotion and the air quivered with tension and unspoken words.

Then he kissed her, a hungry, passionate, heart-thrilling kiss that left her breathless and longing for more. But he withdrew from her, stepping back and taking a package from a shelf.

"I brought you a present," he said, handing it to her.

"Thank you." Her voice was unsteady. The package was heavy and flat in her hands. She unwrapped it and found a large picture book. *The Art of Ikebana*, it said on the glossy cover. The photos of Japanese flower arrangements inside were breathtakingly beautiful. She lowered herself on one of the chairs and slowly looked through the book, marveling at the graceful lines and deceptively simple designs, completely enthralled.

"Oh, Kane, this is gorgeous," she whispered. "I've never seen a book like this." It was written in both Japanese and English and explained each arrangement in detail, giving delicately drawn illustrations of the various steps, from beginning to end of the completed composition.

Finally she put the book down and came to her feet. She moved toward him and wrapped her arms around him. "Thank you," she said. It seemed inadequate somehow. "It was nice of you to think about me."

He laugh was low and incredulous. "Nice? Nice? You say the strangest things. What choice did I have? I've thought of little but you for the past three weeks." He tilted her face upward and kissed her and she wrapped her arms around the solid strength of him. It felt so good to hold him, so good to feel his mouth on hers.

"I promised you a steak," he whispered against her lips. He began to move her backward in the direction of the kitchen. "Come and help me."

And of course the steak was cooked to perfection, and the play they went to see afterwards was wonderfully funny, a perfect choice. She was having a marvelous time, feeling positively elegant in Suzanne's silk dress and the silky hose that had cost a fortune but were worth every penny. Even her nails were clean. She'd worn gloves while she worked the week before, which was a real sacrifice. She'd soaked her hands and scrubbed them and creamed them and they were quite presentable now.

In his elegant dark suit, Kane looked like a different man; urbane, sophisticated, the man she'd met that first day as he stood in her muddy garden with his shiny shoes. His appearance evoked visions of a life she'd once rejected—the gatherings of the powerful, the rich, the beautiful. She thought again of the New York life he had described to her: the gallery openings, the receptions, the art exhibitions, the parties he had to attend. She wondered what it would be like to be married to Kane.

After they got back to the apartment later that night, he poured them each a glass of wine. They sat close together on the big, comfortable couch and she thought of the guest room where she had changed her clothes. She didn't want to sleep there tonight. She leaned her head against Kane's shoulder and sighed.

"Tired?"

"No. I had a good time tonight. I haven't been out for ages. I was beginning to think the world evolved around carrots and fertilizer."

"Very dangerous. We'd better do something about that."

"You're going to take charge of my cultural enrichment?"

"Only as long as you enjoy it."

"Oh, I will, believe me."

He smiled into her eyes, took the glass from her fingers and put it on the table. He leaned toward her and she closed her eyes, feeling his mouth close over hers in a gentle kiss.

"Do you enjoy this?" he asked.

"Yes, but I don't think it's called cultural enrichment."

He laughed softly. "How about sensual enrichment?"

"Mmm." She put her arms around him. "Enrich me some more."

His hands cradled her head and his lips caressed her forehead, her temples, her cheeks with feather-light touches. Then, with a soft moan, he took her mouth again and the gentleness changed into fire and his hands searched restlessly over her body.

Her blood sang. She kissed him back with an urgency of her own, her body trembling with sweet desire. *I love him,* she thought. *I love him.* She could feel the heat of his body through the thin silk of her dress. Her hands moved over the broad expanse of his back, feeling the tension in his muscles.

"Jennifer," he muttered. "Jennifer..." He let out a tortured breath and sat upright. He rubbed the back of his neck. "My God," he groaned. "I can't even kiss you or I go crazy."

"Don't stop. Please don't stop." She pulled him to her, but he took her hands and gently straightened away.

"You'd better go to sleep," he said quietly.

Tears burned behind her lids. "Kane, please make love to me."

He shook his head. "No, Jennifer." The words came with difficulty.

"Why? Don't you want me?"

"Oh, Jennifer, I want you! You know that. I want you so much, I hardly think of anything else when I'm with you."

"Then why don't you make love to me? Why do you always pull back? What's wrong?" Tears ran down her cheeks and she wiped them away impatiently. The fear was back.

"Nothing's wrong. Oh, sweetheart, don't cry." He drew her into his arms with a groan.

"It's your wife, isn't it?" Her voice was muffled against his chest. His body grew still.

"My wife?"

"You want her. You don't really want anybody but her."

He drew away from her very slowly, tilted her chin. "Look at me," he said softly.

She swallowed hard. Through her tears, his face was a blur.

"When you're in my arms, it's you I want. When I kiss you, it's you I want. Please, Jennifer, believe me."

She wanted to. She wanted to believe it with all her heart.

"Then why don't you make love to me? What is it that holds you back?"

He closed his eyes briefly, then looked at her with a strange expression. "I don't want an affair with you, Jennifer."

She was silent for a moment. "What is it that you want then?" she asked softly.

He gave a rueful smile. "The real thing. Love, intimacy, commitment, marriage."

The real thing. It's what he had had with his wife. And he wanted it again. A shared life, love, intimacy, commitment.

"It's too soon for all that."

"I know. It takes time." He brushed her lips with his mouth. "We'll just give it time, all right? Until we are sure of ourselves and of each other."

She nodded.

"I don't want you to get hurt. I don't want us to make a mistake. I want it to be right between us."

"Yes." She wanted it to be right, too. She wanted a future, not some temporary delight that would end in misery. She kissed him, holding him very tight for a moment. "Let's make it right," she whispered.

The next day, it all went wrong.

They'd returned to Guilford and dealt with the paperwork concerning the job. Afterward they'd gone back to the house to see the cleared grounds, which looked twice as large now that all the excess greenery had been taken away.

Kane was pleased with what she had done—pleased and impressed, it was easy to tell from his expression. Pride and elation gave her a sense of euphoria and she could feel herself smile, could hear the lightness in her voice.

"You did an enormous amount of work," he said with respect in his voice.

"I'm enjoying it. It's so exciting now that I'm actually starting the layout and the planting." She sighed and smiled at the same time. "You won't recognize it come fall."

He was silent for a moment as he studied her face. He put his hands on her shoulders. "Jennifer," he said quietly, "if you had a degree, you could do this all the time."

Her heart sank with a crash. Suddenly the joy had gone out of the day and angry resentment rose to the surface.

"I don't want to go back to college," she said numbly.

"Why not?" The compelling look in his eyes demanded an answer—an answer that would satisfy. She knew she had none to give.

She closed her eyes briefly and the anger mingled with fear. "Kane, I told you, I'm happy with what I'm doing. Why can't you accept that?"

"What you like doing is landscaping gardens and that's not what you're doing most of the time."

"Often enough."

"Why don't you like college?"

She gave a frustrated sigh. "I don't like the idea of sitting in stuffy classrooms for years to come and spending my nights poring over books on soil science and hydrology and irrigation and engineering principles and God knows what else. I want to be outside, doing the real work, getting my hands dirty."

"If you had a degree—"

"I don't want a degree! Don't you understand that? I just don't care! I'm not that ambitious! I'm sorry if that offends you, but that's the way it is!"

"It's not lack of ambition, Jennifer," he said slowly, carefully. "It's lack of courage. You're afraid and I'd like to know why."

She jumped to her feet, wild with anger. "I'm not afraid of anything! And I resent you saying these things!" Her legs were shaking and her heart felt heavy with misery. She wanted to stop, but she couldn't. The words kept coming pouring out with the turbulence of her feelings. "You have no right to push your own ideas and expectations on me! You're no different from my parents and my sister! I'm not good enough in their eyes, or in yours! Growing vegetables just doesn't do it—not for them, and not for you, either!" Her voice was high with pain and anger. "You're trying to change me! I don't want to change! I am who I am and you can take it or leave it!"

She turned and jumped down the steps and marched away, around the house to the front, down the driveway and through the gate, her vision blurred with furious tears. Moments later she heard the car behind her, then it stopped next to her and he jumped out and caught her by the arm.

"Let go of me!"

He opened the door. "Get in."

"I'll walk!"

"Don't be stupid." He practically lifted her up and dumped her in the passenger seat and slammed the door shut.

She had no energy to fight him. She huddled against the door, face averted and frozen with outrage and indignation as he drove her home.

It would never work. He would never accept her the way she was. He didn't even want to call her by her name. He wanted to mold her into something else, a more successful person, a professional. That was the sort of person he always dealt with in New York, just like her parents and her sister. Running a little nursery didn't make it by their standards.

Well, to hell with them and their standards! The only standard that mattered was her own. To hell with Kane. She didn't need him. She didn't need any of them!

Kane stopped in front of Jenny's house and before the car had come to a complete stop she'd opened the door, jumped out and slammed it shut again without a word of good-bye. He watched her walk up to the house, noticing the confident swing of her hips in the denim shorts. She held her head proud and high, not looking back once. Damn, that woman had a temper!

He'd better let her cool off for a while, he decided. Maybe by tomorrow she'd have calmed down. He didn't know why suddenly he felt a twinge of fear.

She didn't want to go back to college. He wondered why. She certainly didn't lack the brains. It was like touching a raw nerve when he mentioned it. Well, he was going to find out and if she wanted to throw tantrums, then so be it.

He didn't see how she kept body and soul together running a little nursery in a small town. The property taxes alone would be a fair chunk of her income. How long did she think she could keep it up?

He turned into his drive, looking at the house with satisfaction as he drew nearer. It had a fresh coat of paint, the shutters had been repaired and broken windows replaced. The place was beginning to look like something, he thought, and the garden ... Ah, that garden!

Jennifer tossed in bed and sighed. Something had awakened her, she wasn't sure what. It was raining, a soft, steady dripping that was wonderful for the garden. She listened to the pitter-patter on the bushes outside the window. Surely that had not roused her from sleep. She yawned, turned then stretched, and her feet felt something cold and wet. Instinctively she pulled them back. Then, slowly, she extended her legs again. The end of the bed was wet. Sopping wet.

She sat bolt upright, switched on the bedside lamp and looked at the covers. At the foot end, the quilt showed a dark, circular stain. It was wet, no doubt about it. Now, too, she heard the slow dripping of water. Looking up, she noticed where it came through. There was a dark, wet spot on the ceiling.

She closed her eyes. I'm only dreaming, she thought. There can't possibly be a leak in the roof.

Of course there could be a leak in the roof. The house was old. How old? She didn't even know. Her grandparents had lived in it forever.

I can't afford a leak in the roof, she thought helplessly.

Unfortunately, nobody cared. The leak was there. It was called reality.

Maybe it's only a matter of a tile, she told herself hopefully. One small tile. She could fix it herself. Get Billy James to sell her one sole leftover tile.

Keep dreaming, she jibed herself. If it were a matter of one single roof tile, it wouldn't be leaking straight through the ceiling of the bedroom. There was an attic yet. The water had found its way through the roof and the attic floor and the bedroom ceiling. Not good. Not good at all. Who could tell how long it had been leaking in the attic before it came through the bedroom ceiling? If there was any serious damage at all, she could say good-bye to the money she was making landscaping Kane's garden. She'd be back at point zero.

Kane. Oh, God. The pain rushed back, hot and fierce, burning behind her eyes. It had all been a fantasy after all, a dream that could never come true. This was reality—a man who could not accept her for what she was, a man who wanted to change her. Reality was a broken heart and a leaking roof all in one go.

I'll just have to have a look in the morning, she thought. Crawl on top of the roof, get into the attic. Assess the damage.

But first she needed sleep. Which was a joke. Kane's face haunted her, and apart from that how was she going to sleep with financial disaster hanging over her head, literally? She glared up at the ceiling. Damn, damn!

In a fury Jenny jumped out of bed, dragging the covers with her. Then she dumped them back on. They were wet. They were going to be just as wet on the living room couch. She pushed the bed out of the way and put a plastic bucket under the leak. Picking up her pillow, she left the room, closing the door behind her.

She pulled an old blanket out of the hall closet and went into the living room, switching on the light. Three-thirteen. Turning off the light again she lay down on the couch. It was old and not too comfortable. Everything was old in this house. One by one everything would fall apart. It was not a comforting thought.

Sleep eluded her and morning took ages to come. The rain stopped and she listened to the silence. When the birds began their morning song, she gave up and went to the kitchen to make some breakfast, skipping her customary morning walk.

The work in the greenhouse taken care of, she decided the time had come to inspect the roof. The perfect job for a quiet Sunday morning. She got out the ladder, tightened the laces on her sneakers and climbed up onto the sloping roof. She'd never been up there before and it wasn't easy to keep her balance.

It wasn't hard to find the problem. Even with her layman's eyes it was easy to see that the roof had seen better days. The shingles were weathered and rotten in places. Some had disappeared completely, blown off by a spring storm probably. She sat down and took a deep breath. You're in trouble, old girl, she told herself with mock cheer. This is going to cost you a bundle. Every cent you're making doing Kane's garden. She sat down, dejected.

The morning breeze blew against her hot cheeks. The world this sunny Sunday morning was very quiet. She looked out over the fields, the dark woods and hills in the distance. A beautiful sight from her high perch, but she was in no mood to enjoy it.

Carefully she made her way back down. Now for the attic.

It wasn't an actual storage attic and she'd never been up there. Armed with a flashlight she hoisted herself up through a trapdoor into the warm, gloomy space. The sight that greeted her there was equally discouraging. The roof had obviously been leaking for quite some time and a large area of the floor showed rot and decay. Getting it fixed again would take a considerable repair job.

She thought of Billy James. He wasn't a building contractor, but he was capable handyman. At the very least she should ask his advice. She called him at the shop, after she knew it had opened. "It's Jenny, Billy. I've got a problem. A leak in my roof."

"You want me to have a look at it?"

"I'd appreciate that, yes. I checked it out myself and it looks pretty bad. I'm not sure what I should do about it."

"All right, I'll drop by later this afternoon. The shop is a zoo right now."

"Sure, fine. I'll be here."

He came later that afternoon and the news was bad. She needed a whole new roof and a new beam in the attic floor.

A whole new roof. Structural damage in the attic. It was even worse than she had expected. She took him into the bedroom and showed him the ceiling.

In the end there's always you, wailed the radio in the kitchen, a new country and western song she must have heard a dozen times in the past few days.

"You'll need a couple of new ceiling boards," Billy said. "No big problem." He frowned. "I think you should have Caster in town replace that beam in the attic. It could've leaked there for years and I don't want to fool with it. I can do the roof for you and the ceiling. If you want me to."

He pulled up a chair, stood on it and poked the ceiling with his finger. It went straight through the sodden plaster-board, and pieces of it crumbled and fell down on the floor. The chair creaked ominously. Oh, Lord, she thought in horror, he shouldn't be standing on that chair! Before she could utter a warning, the chair collapsed under Billy's considerable weight and, with his hands flailing, he fell off sideways, taking Jenny with him in his fall. They both landed on the rug in a heap of tangled arms and legs. For a moment, they stared at each other in stunned silence. Then Jenny began to laugh, as she realized the ridiculous picture they were making. She sat up and rubbed her leg. It was nothing serious and Billy seemed to be all in one piece.

"I'm sorry. I should have told you not to stand on that old chair. It's my fault."

"Forget it." He was laughing too, reaching for her hand to help her up.

I'm often sad, I'm often blue, but in the end there's always you, the radio wailed.

And then she saw Kane.

He was standing in the bedroom door, eyes steely with restrained anger.

"What's going on here?" he demanded.

Jenny stood up, wiping her hands on her jeans. She resented his tone of voice. "I don't believe I invited you in," she said coolly.

"I knocked and I called, but you didn't hear me."

"The radio was on," she said unnecessarily, and the refrain jangled through the air once more.

Billy looked uneasily at Kane. He wiped at the bits of plaster on his shirt. "I'd better go now. Let me know what you decide, Jenny." He moved to the door and Kāne stepped aside to let him pass.

For a moment there was silence as Kane's gaze swept around the chaos in the room—the bed moved out of place, the broken chair, the pieces of wet ceiling board on the floor.

"What was he doing here?" he asked then.

"I would think it's obvious. I have a leak and I asked him to check it out. Not that it is any of your business." She turned her back to him and began to pick up the pieces of the chair.

He grasped her arm and swung her toward him. "Don't you know any better than to ask men into your house while you're here alone?"

His tone infuriated her and she yanked her arm free. Who did he think he was, talking to her like that? Why didn't he mind his own business instead of meddling in hers? Did he think he could push her around, tell her what to do with her life and whom to invite into her house? Well, he had another think coming!

"I've known Billy James for years," she said acidly. "He's a handyman and he's helped me out on several occasions."

"From what I saw, it must be a very cozy arrangement."

The color drained from her face and a cold rage rushed through her.

"Get out!" she whispered fiercely. "Get out of my house!" To her horror, tears filled her eyes.

He came toward her, his face pale. "Jennifer..."

"Just get away from me!" Turning round, she threw herself on the bed, burying her face in the pillow.

"Jennifer..."

"Go away!"

He pulled her upright, both arms clamped around her so she couldn't move. "I apologize," he said quietly. "I'm sorry, I really am. I don't know what made me say it. I was so furious, I didn't know what I was saying. The way he looked at you, I could have strangled him."

She sat rigidly in his arms. "All right, now let me go."

He released her and stood up. His eyes were bleak and he observed her for a long, silent moment. Then he glanced up at the ceiling.

"I'll send somebody over to have a look at that leak," he said.

She clenched her hands into fists, forcing herself to stay calm. "Don't bother," she said coldly, "I can take care of it myself. I don't need your help. I don't need your protection. And I don't need your career counseling."

Jaw rigid, he looked down at her with dark, unreadable eyes. "As you please." He turned on his heel and strode out of the room.

She was still standing near the bed when she heard the car drive away. Then the phone began to ring and with heavy legs she moved to the office and lifted the receiver.

"Hello?"

"Jenny? It's me, Mary. I've got a problem."

"What is it?" She frowned at the urgency in Mary's voice.

"My cabbages have holes in them!"

Jenny closed her eyes, forcing down a hysterical laugh.

Mary's cabbages have holes in them, she said to herself. Who says I have problems?

Chapter Seven

I don't know what I did wrong," Mary moaned. "I swear I did everything you told me to do."

Jenny sat down on a chair, with a sigh. "I'll come over and have a look. I was going to call you and see if I could talk to Tom for a few minutes anyway. I need some financial advice."

"Why don't you come over later today after you close up shop, and stay for dinner? We're only barbecuing hamburgers, but I've got plenty."

"Thanks. I'd like that."

Tom was a loan officer at the local bank. He was a nice guy, though somewhat bland and colorless, but Mary was crazy about him, which was all that mattered. Jenny hoped the bank would give her a short-term loan for the roof. The landscaping job would have to pay for it, but she didn't have all the money yet. The idea of going into debt, even for a couple of months, gave her nightmares, but there was no choice. The roof needed fixing. That was the long and the short of it. But in the back of her mind unease stirred and a refrain started jangling through her head . . . *the beginning of the end, the beginning of the end.*

Kane was going back to New York that afternoon. Her heart felt like it had a hole in it and every time she thought of him there was nothing but pain and regret. Dammit, why had she fallen in love with a man who was so obviously wrong for her? He could never be happy with someone like her. He needed a woman with more drive, more ambition. A woman more like himself.

But she wasn't. And so he was trying to change her. Just like her parents and Suzanne had always tried to change her.

Suzanne. She closed her eyes and she could no longer push back the anger welling up in her. She'd never been as smart or as popular or as beautiful as her sister. She'd disappointed her parents. Oh, her grades had always been fine, and she'd gotten herself into a good college and earned a respectable B.A. and had been working on her master's in education. But a career in education wasn't what she'd wanted. She hadn't known what she had wanted. She'd had no great desire or calling, no burning passion for one thing or another.

And then her grandfather had died and left her the nursery and things had changed. She was determined to keep the nursery running. Some of her happiest times had been spent there with her grandfather. He was the only one who had not expected her to be any different than she was, the only one who had not demanded she do better or more. He had loved her the way she was. She wanted to keep the feelings alive, not lose a part of her childhood that she cherished.

Her parents had been furious, Suzanne sarcastic and offensive. She didn't care. She was going to do what she wanted to do and nobody was going to change her mind. She was fed up doing what she was supposed to do—be a good girl, listen to Daddy, keep her room clean, dress neatly, smile politely, be a lady, finish grad school, do something brilliant like her sister.

To hell with it all. She was going to run the nursery and play in the mud and get dirty.

And here she was, doing just that. The house was a mess, her nails were broken, the roof was leaking and she had no money for repairs.

"You don't look very cheerful," Mary commented, when Jenny arrived later that afternoon. She was standing at the kitchen counter, mixing up one of her elaborate salad dressings.

"That's because I've got nothing to be cheerful about," Jenny answered glumly, staring at the jars of herbs and spices on the counter.

"Oh?" Mary's eyebrows rose, making her face look even thinner and longer. "You've got the job of your life—landscaping the Cleever house grounds—and, I believe, a promising relationship with the owner."

Jenny shrugged. "Well, yeah . . ."

Mary looked at her and frowned. "What do you mean, well, yeah? You always wanted to do those grounds!" She paused a fraction of a moment. "Something wrong between you and Kane?"

"You could say that." Jenny sighed and sat down on a stool. "My relationship with Kane is doomed, and I woke up this morning and my bed was soaking wet."

Mary goggled at her. *"What?"*

"From a leak in the roof," she added, managing a half smile. "Billy James had a look at it and said I need a new beam in the attic and a whole new roof."

Mary grimaced. "Oh, boy. Hence the search for financial advice." She shook the jar with dressing vigorously.

"I'm hoping the bank will give me a short-term loan."

"They probably will. Tom will know. Here, taste this." Mary dribbled a few drops of the dressing on Jenny's hand. "Does it need anything else?"

Jenny licked her hand. "Maybe a bit more lemon juice. It's good, though."

"Okay, here goes." Mary squeezed a cut lemon over the jar. "Damn, a pit. Oh, well, never mind."

"You'd better fish it out," Jenny advised. "The way things are going, I'll get it in my salad and break a tooth on it."

Mary barely suppressed a grin. "I've never seen you so down."

With an effort, Jenny squared her shoulders and courageously pasted on a bright smile. "It's only a temporary deviation. I'll soon be my old, cheerful self again. All I need is to win the lottery and send in my broken heart for repairs. I hear they have magical new bonding techniques these days."

"Are you ladies ready?" Tom stood in the kitchen door, waving a spatula as if it were a baseball bat. "The hamburgers are done."

"So are we." Mary picked up the bowl of salad and the dressing. "Jenny, grab the iced tea out of the fridge, will you?"

The food and the company cheered Jenny up. She fed the baby from a jar and he was in great spirits, smearing the food all over his face and his high chair tray.

Tom didn't think there'd be a problem getting Jenny a home improvement loan since she owned the house and the land outright. This cheered her up even more. He told her to come to the bank the next day and figure it out.

They lingered over the meal, drinking coffee and eating chocolate cake afterward, enjoying the warm evening air.

Later Jenny counseled Mary on the cabbage while Tom went inside to get the baby ready for bed.

"So why is your relationship with Kane not working out?" asked Mary, when they went back into the kitchen to do the dishes. "Or shouldn't I ask?"

"We just don't make a good match. He's very... ambitious, goal-oriented, I guess. He built his own business from scratch and is doing very well. And you know me—I putter around with my flowers and vegetables and I'm perfectly happy. He thinks I should go back to college, study landscape architecture, have a career."

Mary ran hot water into the sink. "And you don't want to?"

"No. I don't see why. I like what I'm doing now. I enjoy being my own boss, doing my own thing. And I'm just not that ambitious."

"If you don't want to go back to college, I don't see any reason why you should. Certainly not to please him."

"That's what I think."

"Have you told him?"

"Oh, sure! But he just won't give up. He keeps bringing up the subject."

"He has no right to push you, Jenny."

"I've said that, too. We had a terrible argument. I told him that I am who I am and he could take it or leave it."

Mary grinned. "Good for you."

"So why do I feel so miserable?" She picked up a plate and began to dry it.

"You're disillusioned."

"You can say that again. I just wish he'd accept me the way I am. But he can't imagine not wanting more out of life than I have. He can't see that I'm happy the way I am. What he needs, of course, is a career woman, somebody just like him."

Mary frowned, looking thoughtful. "You can only live by your own standards, Jenny. You have to be yourself. So whatever you do, don't let him push you into doing something you don't want to do. You'll only resent it later and be even more miserable."

"I know, believe me. I've spent years resenting my parents for pushing me to do what I didn't want to do." It was a comfort to know at least one person was on her side. She picked up a coffee cup. "How about coming to the Cleever house sometime to see what I've done?"

"I'd love to. I've been wanting to do that for a while. I'm sure it's going to be wonderful."

Jenny put the cup on the counter and smiled. "It is, it really is."

As she drove home, she wondered if her parents would ever come to see the place. She hadn't been home for several weeks now. There was so much work to be done, she hardly had time for anything else.

Jenny did get the loan, with the house as collateral, and a short time later the house had a new roof and the rest of the damage had been repaired as well.

Over the next several weeks she saw little of Kane, who seemed to travel often and came only now and then to check up on the house and to talk to her about the garden. He was polite and businesslike and she kept her distance, forcing back the pain and the longing she felt every time she was near him. It was no use. There was a hard knot of misery in her chest, growing harder every time she saw him. All the sweetness had gone out of life, the laughter, the pleasure. Her body still ached for his touch and he would come to her in her dreams telling her he loved her and wanted her, and the torture of her nightly fantasies sapped her vitality.

She worked on the grounds every available minute, putting into it all she had, all her imagination and creativity and ingenuity. She took time finding the right plants and shrubs, ground covers and flowers, selecting some unusual ones as well as the more common varieties. It took time and deliberation to make reality out of the design on paper. Minor changes had to be made, but she was delighted that no major problems arose. She'd done her homework well, and it paid off.

She'd hired a number of local people to help her and it was working out very well. There was a lot of hard work to be done, but she didn't mind that. She loved seeing the bare, cleared land change into something beautiful before her eyes. Kane's garden was her baby, her grand design, her glory.

She was at work one Friday evening when she saw the gray Continental come up the driveway. Kane was at the wheel and a woman was sitting next to him. Jenny was hidden from their view by a grouping of pines and as the car passed by her, she caught a gleam of red hair and a laughing mouth. Never before had she experienced such instant, hot jealousy, such piercing fear. Rooted to the ground she stared at Kane as he got out of the car and opened the door for the woman. With his arm around her shoulders he led her up the steps and unlocked the front door. They disappeared inside.

Jenny felt sick to her stomach and she wiped her clammy forehead with her hand.

It can't be true, she told herself. *He didn't get himself another woman just like that. He wouldn't.* Well, why not? Hadn't she tried to make it clear to him she wasn't interested any longer? *I don't need your help. I don't need your protection. And I don't need your career counseling.* Her words echoed in her head like an accusation. She'd wanted him to get the message. No doubt he had.

Her mouth was dry and her heart labored with heavy, painful beats. Maybe she wasn't his new woman. Maybe she had something to do with the house, an interior decorator or somebody like that. Maybe this very minute they were going through the house measuring for curtains. But you didn't put your arm around the shoulders of an interior decorator unless she was more than just that. Maybe she was one of his sisters. One of them taught at Columbia and lived in New York. That was probably it. She was here to admire the house.

So, she said to herself, if that's what it is, why don't I feel any better? She looked down at her hands, caked with mud. She'd better finish the job. She was planting the last of the golden hypericum, one of her favorite ground covers. It had showy yellow flowers, exotic, almost tropical-looking blooms that grew lusciously all through the summer.

Kane and the woman came outside again sometime later and started walking down the drive.

"Jennifer?" Kane called.

He had seen the red truck, of course. He'd probably seen her at work from one of the bedroom windows. Damn, she thought as she saw them approach. I look like a disaster. Well, what do I care? She came to her feet, rubbing her hands together to clean off some of the mud. She stepped onto the drive.

"I'm here."

"How is it going?"

Her heart beat erratically. "Fine," she said coolly. She looked at the woman. She was gorgeous, of course. Straight off the streets of Manhattan in the latest fashion. Glorious red hair, beautiful face.

"Jennifer, I want you to meet my sister, Vicky. Vicky, this is Jennifer."

The wave of relief that flooded her made her knees weak. I must be crazy, she thought. Why do I react like this? She smiled at Vicky, who extended her hand. Jenny shook her head and grimaced.

"You don't want to shake hands with me. I'm filthy. But I'm glad to meet you. Kane has told me about you."

Vicky's smile was open and friendly. "And he has told me about you, too. I'd love to see what you've done with this garden. Will you show me around?"

She didn't mind in the least. She felt an instant liking for her. Maybe because she's no threat, Jenny told herself cynically. If she'd been somebody else you'd hate her on sight. They walked around, the three of them, Jenny doing most of the talking, explaining to Vicky about the way she had landscaped the grounds, about the shrubs she had planted— the azaleas and lilacs and the two dozen rosebushes. And as she talked, she forgot everything else. This was her domain, here she was in her element, and it was after some time she realized that Kane had not said a word and was observing her with a keen intensity. Had he been looking at her all this time, watching her as she talked?

"Well," she said abruptly. "I think I'd better go home now. It's beginning to get dark. It was nice meeting you, Vicky. I'll see you around, Kane." She walked off, got into the pickup and put the key into the ignition. Her hand was trembling.

"Don't stall on me now," she muttered as she turned the key. It had been stalling more and more lately. Something was not right.

"So what else is new," she said out loud. Something wasn't right with the damn truck, but it wasn't the only thing. Her whole life seemed wrong these days. She put the car in gear, slowly let out the clutch and drove home, fighting tears. She didn't want to cry. There was nothing to cry about. Nothing.

Kane came to see her early the next morning before she was open for business. She was arranging the sprinklers in the vegetable garden. It had been unusually dry and the new plants needed water. She saw him coming and her heart played its tricks on her again and began to beat frantically. His pace was easy and unhurried, his thumbs hooked through the belt loops of his jeans. His white T-shirt seemed molded to his body, making no secret of the broad shoulders and wide chest. She bit her lip hard and pretended not to see him.

"Good morning, Jennifer."

"Good morning." She didn't look at him, but continued with her work.

"Jennifer? I want to talk to you."

She glanced up. "Is there a problem with the garden?"

"No."

She picked up a hose and dragged it around. "What, then?"

He followed her as she pulled another hose between the pumpkin plants and adjusted the sprinkler.

"Can you leave that damned hose alone for a minute and talk to me?"

She straightened up slowly, seeing the irritation in his eyes. "What did you want to talk about?" she asked politely.

"About you and me."

"There's nothing to say."

"I want you to come into the city with me next week. I'm having a party—a reception, actually."

She stared at him. A *party*? He had to be kidding. "No, thank you," she said evenly. The last thing she wanted was to stand around at a reception and shake hands with the bright and beautiful who'd come to case out each other.

His mouth was a grim line and anger sparked in his eyes. "Jennifer, I've had about all I can take! I don't want to go on this way!"

She shrugged. "I don't know what you mean."

His jaw grew rigid. "Oh, yes, you do! We're hurting each other. For weeks now you've barely been civil to me. You look like hell. I feel like hell. I want this to stop!"

She clenched her hands. "We're not right for each other. It was all a mistake. You don't like me the way I am and I can't change myself. I won't! We should just forget it."

"I don't want to forget it! And I don't think you want to either!"

She squared her shoulders and glared at him. "You don't know anything about what I want!" She couldn't stand his presumptuous attitude.

"I know what you feel, Jennifer. Yesterday, when you saw Vicky...don't you think I know what you were thinking? I saw your face when you looked at her. Don't tell me you don't care, because you'd be lying. I want this nonsense to stop. I don't want this anger and hostility between us. You've given me the cold shoulder for weeks now and I'm losing my patience! I can't take it. We have to figure this out somehow."

Her stomach churned with anxiety. She took a steadying breath. "You make me feel as if I'm not good enough! As if my work here at the nursery isn't worth anything. But you're just going to have to take me the way I am!" Her voice shook. "I don't want you criticizing me or telling me what I should do with my life!"

He rubbed his chin and frowned. "Jennifer..."

"Why can't you just let me be?" she cried. "What's wrong with me the way I am? Why can't you just let me be?"

He came a step closer and she saw the fire in his eyes as he leaned toward her. "Because it goes against everything I do and believe! I've been all over the world looking for art and talent. Art is to be seen and enjoyed, not hidden on some small island or in some remote village. Art needs light and recognition. Talent needs to be used, Jennifer, not hidden. I see all this potential in you, mostly unused. And it bothers me. Don't you understand that?"

She didn't want to hear what he was saying, yet the words registered and took on meaning and she revolted. "I'm not an artist, for heaven's sake! All I do is plan gardens and plant shrubs!"

"And that doesn't take talent? Oh, but you're wrong there, Jennifer! Not many have the eye for shape and color and design that you have. You have a marvelous imagination, a creativity that shines through that whole garden out there, and it's not even finished!"

"You're making too much of it, Kane."

He shook his head slowly. "No, Jennifer, you're not making enough of it!"

She closed her eyes. "I don't want to talk about it anymore."

He sighed. "Oh, Jennifer!" He reached out to her, but she stepped back, avoiding him. She stared at him, her throat aching and her eyes burning with unshed tears. She saw the raw pain in his eyes as he slowly lowered his arms by his sides.

"Can't we call a truce, please?" he asked.

"I don't want you telling me what to do."

He gave a sigh of resignation. "All right."

She looked at him warily. His face looked tired, his mouth weary, as if he hadn't smiled in a long time.

"Jennifer," he said softly, "it's been hell these last few weeks. I love you. I need you."

Her heart made a somersault. He had never told her he loved her and she had longed to hear those words. Her throat closed and tears blurred her vision.

He came a step closer, but didn't touch her. "Let me hold you, please."

And then she was in his arms, tears streaming down her face, his hands tangled in her hair.

"Oh, God, I'm sorry, Jennifer. I don't want anything to ruin what we have together. I'm not going to let it." His mouth roamed over her face and throat. "I love you, I want you. I dream of you every damned night and I can't sleep." His hands cradled her face and he pulled back a little to look into her eyes. "You're pigheaded and stubborn and beautiful and talented and I want you in my life. I can't live without hearing your voice and seeing that funny smile of yours." He drew her face closer and his mouth was hot and feverish and the heat of it flushed her body.

"I love you, too," she whispered. "Oh, Kane, I love you, too."

She made coffee while Kane made a pile of toast and they put it on a tray with butter and honey and carried it out to the back porch and put it on the weathered wooden table.

"You're sure you want me at that party next Saturday?" she asked.

"Absolutely! I want to show you off. You're a rare find."

She gaped at him. "Show me off? Rare find? You make me sound like I'm one of your possessions, a piece of art on your wall."

His grin held no apology. "I didn't think I'd get away with that."

"Darn right you won't!" She slathered butter onto a piece of toast and drizzled honey on it. "I want you to know that I'm going under duress. I don't like big parties."

"Why not?"

"I used to go to functions and cocktail parties when I still lived with my parents. They are very much out there on the social circuit. I hate all that phoniness, the one-upmanship. Who has the biggest case, the most beautiful mistress, the most expensive dress? And the business deals everybody is after, all that power-brokering. I always had to be so careful what I said and to whom. Someone was always out there to get you." She smiled ruefully. "Do I sound paranoid?"

"Definitely. And you'll be pleasantly surprised at my party. Only nice people are allowed."

"It'll be very interesting to see," she said with some measure of doubt.

"I want my friends to meet you, and vice versa. They knew about the house, of course, and I've told them about you doing the landscaping. Actually, I bragged about you quite considerably." He gave a boyish grin and Jenny couldn't help but smile back.

"You told them I could get quite considerably dirtier than anybody you've ever known." She bit hungrily into the toast.

"Something like that." There were laughing lights in his eyes. "Oh, and I was thinking of something else. I'd like to meet your parents."

"Oh," she said, caught off guard.

"Don't you want me to meet them? I'm curious. Especially about your mother. You told me she's the Wicked Witch of the West. I've never met a witch."

Jenny laughed. "Don't tell her I told you. And I'm sure they'd be delighted to meet you. Sunday dinner some time? Maybe next week, the day after the party?"

He nodded. "I'd like that."

"I'll call home and arrange it."

They finished their breakfast in contented leisure. It was a peaceful summer morning filled with sunshine and the song of birds. A breeze stirred the leaves of the big oak tree and they watched a couple of squirrels chase each other across the grass.

At ten sharp the first customer drove up the drive and reluctantly Jenny got up to help him. When she came back, Kane was in the kitchen washing the dishes.

"Thanks," she said. He turned and took her in his arms and kissed her lightly. "You taste like honey."

"I wonder why. Mm, kiss me some more."

His eyes grew dark. "I'm sorry I can't stay today, but I have to take Vicky back this afternoon after I talk to the contractor and tomorrow I'm taking off again until next Friday."

Disappointment was heavy in her chest, but she tried not to show it. "Where are you going?"

"Venezuela. Not a bad trip, but I wish I didn't have to go." He kissed her again, hard and almost desperate this time, then he let go. "I'll see you next week." He turned and strode out the kitchen. Jenny watched him through the window, a lump in her throat.

He wouldn't mention her going back to school again. He wouldn't talk about her getting a degree. She sighed as she turned away from the window.

Why didn't she believe him?

If only I can make it through this summer.

Kane leaned back in his seat and closed his eyes. He

couldn't take another plane trip, another stay in an impersonal hotel room, meals alone in restaurants. And after each trip he'd come home to an empty apartment. He'd had enough of it all.

Once the summer was over he'd have time, plenty of time to deal with that stubborn woman in Guilford. He smiled thinking about her, seeing again the angry blue eyes in the tanned face. Saturday morning he'd watched her for some time as she arranged the sprinklers in her garden, enjoying the sight of her in her shorts and shirt, long slim legs moving easily over the uneven ground, brown arms gleaming in the sun. Her hair was bleached almost white, her face free of makeup. She looked the picture of womanly wholesomeness, fit and healthy and suntanned. She belonged there in the garden, amid the plants and the flowers and the trees, with the blue sky reflected in her eyes and the birds twittering in the trees.

She'd transformed the jungle around his house into a paradise, or at least the beginnings of one. It was incredible what she had done in such a short time and he was constantly amazed at her handiwork. *You're making too much of it,* she'd said. How could she possibly not want to develop her talent? He could tell by the expression in her eyes how much the work meant to her. In the garden, talking, working, she came alive. Her face would glow, her eyes would shine with eagerness, her whole being would radiate energy and enthusiasm. He loved watching her, marveling at what went on in her mind.

"Would you like a drink, sir?" The flight attendant smiled down at him with perfectly outlined lips. He thought of Jennifer's mouth, naturally soft and pink and usually free of lipstick. He smiled at the woman in front of him.

"Vodka, please. Straight."

She poured him the drink and handed it over along with a tiny foil bag of roasted almonds. Her fingernails were long and polished a deep, shiny pink. Her hands looked delicate and artificial to him, something he would never have thought until he'd met Jennifer. Jennifer with the muddy hands. Nails clipped short. Small, capable hands that were creating miracles in his garden at this very moment. She was self-conscious about her hands, he knew. Often she'd hide them behind her back so he wouldn't see them. Yet she didn't wear gloves unless she needed them to keep herself from getting hurt. Like the time she had been moving railroad ties. She'd used the ties cleverly to terrace a steep area that would have otherwise been difficult to handle and he'd come upon her and the men as they were working. She'd worked right along with the men, carrying and shifting the heavy ties to get them in the right places, wielding a hammer to force in the gigantic nails that kept the structure from shifting.

He would never get enough of looking at her, seeing her small, strong body move around as she worked, the muscles tensing and relaxing in her calves and arms and back, the blue eyes full of concentration. How much more beautiful she was than any of the women he knew in New York, with their faces hidden behind masks of makeup, their artificial smiles and perfectly groomed hair. He swallowed some vodka and smiled at himself. Well, that wasn't fair. He was exaggerating. Certainly Vicky was no artificial person, despite her beautiful clothes and the use of makeup. And neither had been his wife.

Anne. He shifted in his seat and stared out the little window, seeing nothing but white clouds like fluffy cotton floating in a sea of blue sky. He had loved her more than he had loved anybody. He had missed her with deepest, darkest despair. Their life together was over, had been over for years now, yet in his mind she had always been with him.

It was time to let go. Time to start over, to make emotional investments in a new and different future.

He remembered the day he had first met Jennifer, the time Vicky had come to his apartment to be with him. *It's the twenty-seventh*, she'd said. The day Anne had died four years ago. And he'd forgotten. He remembered the guilt he had felt. But he didn't feel guilty any longer.

Anne would be the last to want that from him. She had loved him and no doubt she'd want him to be happy again and not mourn her death till the end of his days. Still, there would always be the pain and regret for the loss of their dreams, the loss of a son that had shattered something deep inside his soul which time would never heal.

The attendant asked him for his choice of dinner, spread a white cloth on his table and poured him some wine.

"Have you taken this flight before?" she asked, looking at him intently. "You look familiar." There was an unmistakable invitation in her eyes.

"Not recently," he said politely, noticing the instant withdrawal in her face. The smile now was purely professional.

"I must have confused you with someone else," she said, stepping back to tend to another traveler. Kane shrugged mentally.

He just wasn't interested.

Chapter Eight

I'm back."

Jenny smiled into the phone, feeling ridiculous joy at the sound of Kane's voice. "I'm glad. How was your trip?"

"A mixed pleasure. I kept wishing you were with me."

"And I kept wishing you were here."

"I will be tomorrow. I have some business with the contractor and then I'll pick you up. You haven't changed your mind about the party, have you?"

She laughed. "No. And my parents are looking forward to meeting you on Sunday."

Shortly after one the next afternoon, the gray Continental stopped in front of the house. Jenny ran out to meet him and he lifted her off her feet in a big embrace.

"You do make me feel welcome," he said in her ear and kissed her. A group of teenage boys in a blue junker jeered and whistled as they raced by on the road.

Kane grinned. "They're just jealous." He put his arm around her shoulders and moved toward the house. "Let's get your stuff."

"It's in the kitchen. I'm all ready." There was only one small suitcase and a box and they carried them to the car.

"What's in the box?" Kane asked as he opened up the trunk.

"It's a surprise." Carefully she put the box on the floor in front of the backseat, bracing it so it wouldn't slide back and forth. "I made it especially for you, for the party." She gave him a taunting smile as they settled themselves on the seats.

"Let me guess," he said, starting the car.

"Don't even try."

He laughed. "Now I'm really intrigued."

"You'll just have to wait."

Despite her misgivings, she'd looked forward to the party all week. She hadn't been out for ages and a little diversion was welcome. She'd left the nursery in the care of her part-time helper and everything was under control.

Kane told her of his week in Venezuela and it was relaxing just to sit in the comfortable car and listen and not have a single thing to do. At home she never just sat.

Once inside the apartment, she put the box on the kitchen table and Kane looked at her with narrowed eyes.

"So what's in there? Is it alive?"

She laughed. "Don't look so suspicious and, yes, it is alive." She reached inside the box, carefully took out a flower arrangement and put it on the table. It was assembled in a low oval dish and consisted of only a few flowers and leafy branches. It was her first effort to make a Japanese flower arrangement according to the principles spelled out in the book on ikebana he'd brought her from Japan. It had looked deceptively easy, yet when she'd started work on it she'd realized there was more to it than met the eye. It had taken her a long time to find just the right branches with just the right angles and curves. She had not actually attempted to copy the picture—it would have been impossible—but she'd used her own feeling for line and color and design, and after various aborted attempts, she had come up with something that had pleased her.

"It's beautiful," he said quietly. "A piece of art."

She felt warm with pleasure at his praise. "I liked doing it. But it wasn't easy."

"I know it isn't. It's a very tricky composition. Have you ever done any sculpting or painting?"

"I took a couple of art courses in college. We did a little of everything. I enjoyed it a lot." She looked around the room for a place to put the arrangement. The low, teak coffee table was large and square with clean, simple lines. A large bouquet of white carnations stood in the middle of it.

"I think it would look best on the table," she suggested. "If you don't mind moving the carnations."

"I don't mind. Mrs. DeRosa bought them." He smiled with amusement. "Always puts them right in the middle, too. I'll move them off-center and when I come back home at night they're right back in the middle."

Jenny frowned. "I wonder why."

"There's comfort in symmetry."

She nodded. "Maybe you're right. I hadn't thought about that. I've always found symmetry very boring."

"It usually is. Balance is a lot trickier."

Jenny picked up the arrangement and grimaced. "Tell me about it. You know how long it took me to work this one out?"

"A long time." He took the bowl of carnations and moved them to a side table.

"You're right." She placed the arrangement on the table, shifting it to several places and stepping back to look at the final result. At last she was satisfied.

"What time is everybody coming? Shall I change now?"

He wrapped his arms around her and kissed her. "Yes, go ahead and change." He moved his feet forward, nudging her body to go backward. Locked together they slowly made their way to the bedroom, kissing, almost tripping over each other's feet, laughing.

He began to undo the buttons of her blouse, slowly, teasingly, sliding it off her shoulders at last. She gave him a push.

"Now go. I'm quite capable of taking off my own clothes."

"I never doubted that."

"Kane, get out of here."

He gave her a wicked grin, but obliged, and she took off the rest of her clothes.

Jenny dressed in one of Suzanne's dresses, a soft blue with a shimmery silver thread running through the fabric. It made her look quite sophisticated. She put on an antique silver necklace and matching earrings that had belonged to her grandmother, and with the simple dress they looked just right. She only used a light makeup and her hair was loose, smooth and shiny, swept away from her face and held in place by a silver comb.

"You're gorgeous," Kane said, kissing her. "You're like a different woman in a dress. I'm so used to seeing you in shorts or jeans, I'm not sure you're the same person."

"You like me better this way?" she asked.

His eyes probed hers for a moment. He shook his head. "Not better. I like you any way, shape or form."

Except unambitious and unwilling to get a degree, she thought in automatic response. And the fear was back. It couldn't last, this happiness they had together. It was only an illusion, a temporary joy. They were too different for it to last.

"What's wrong?" His eyes searched her face.

It took an effort to smile. "Nothing, nothing, really."

She could tell he didn't believe her, but he didn't pursue it, much to her relief.

The guests arrived, alone or in twos and threes, all colors, sizes and ages, including a tiny baby whose parents had not yet found the courage to entrust him to a babysitter. He was asleep in a portable bed and after everybody had oohed and ahed over him dutifully he was put into the guest room.

They were just ordinary people, Kane had said. Yet as the evening progressed, Jenny couldn't help but be fascinated.

There were several people who'd made it big with innovative business deals. There was a famous sculptor, a man with a gentle sense of humor and an inordinately modest way about him. "He's something of a recluse," Kane told her. "Doesn't like all the fuss of being famous."

There were others: a woman who'd started her own travel agency; a dealer in oriental antiques and his partner/wife; a filmmaker, Shana, whose wildlife documentaries were well-known for their creative style and scientific integrity.

Success had not come easy, Shana told Jenny as she nibbled on a handful of cashew nuts. It had taken her years before she got her foot in the door, before anybody wanted to air her work. Years of struggle and hard work and poverty and disillusionment.

"So many times I just wanted to give up and get a job at the bank or something," she said, smiling wryly at the memory. "I even tried it once. But I went crazy. I couldn't do it. I just had to make films—I couldn't give it up. I couldn't see myself never making another movie again. So I kept trying."

It wasn't hard to believe. The big gray eyes in the small face were full of determination and the tilt of her chin spoke of stubborn resolve and endless willpower. She wasn't pretty in the traditional sense, but she had an arresting face. She'd dressed in an interesting outfit—silky bloomers with a long tunic hanging loose over them and a scarf draped around her neck. Her father had bought it for her in Pakistan several years earlier, she told Jenny.

Shana took a hearty drink from her glass. "You're about to lose your comb," she added, gesturing at Jenny's head. Jenny reached up to touch the silver comb.

"It keeps doing that. My hair's too heavy, or the comb is too flimsy. I'll go fix it."

She was in the bathroom brushing out her hair when she heard a noise. She listened. The baby? It was very faint. She opened the bathroom door and walked across the hall to the guest bedroom. She'd heard right, the baby was crying. Putting her hand on the doorknob she hesitated for a moment, then saw Kane coming toward her.

"I was looking for—" He stopped as he heard the baby.

"He's crying," she said unnecessarily. "Shall I get his mother?"

Kane stepped inside the room. "Let's see what we can do." He peeked into the bassinet, then reached in and very gently lifted out the baby. Kane cradled him in his arms and looked tenderly down at the tiny face. "Now, now," he said softly, "why all the fuss? Are you hungry? Are you wet? Are you unhappy about the new tax law? Well, I can't blame you. I don't think much of it, either."

Jenny felt a rush of love as she watched the big man holding the tiny baby. Kane was completely at ease, not at all uncomfortable with the diminutive size of the infant.

The baby stopped crying for a moment, then screwed up his little face once more and gave a pitiful wail.

"Okay, okay, so I was wrong. It's not the tax law, after all, but the diaper. That one is easily remedied." He looked over at Jenny. "How about handing me the diaper bag and we'll give this young man a pair of dry britches."

She picked up the bag from the chair. "I'll do it if you like."

"Not necessary. You see before you a very experienced diaper changer."

Jenny thought of his son, who'd been little more than a baby when he'd died, and a painful sadness clogged her throat as she watched Kane.

He laid the baby on the bed and divested him expertly of his sleeper and the sodden diaper. "Good Lord, man," he murmured, "what did you do all day? Drink beer?" In no time at all, he had cleaned and dressed the baby again. Draping the small bundle against his shoulder, he began walking the room with him. "Now, are you going to sleep or do we have to bother your poor mother for a meal? I bet you've been up every night and she hasn't had a good night's rest since you were born." He spoke softly, his voice very tender.

"Maybe there's a bottle. I'll look."

"I doubt it very much. His mother is severely into health food. Nothing adulterated will pass this child's lips until the neighborhood children teach him the delights of gummi bears and chocolate candy bars."

A search of the diaper bag did not produce a bottle of formula. "You're right," she agreed. "No milk here." But the baby had stopped crying and lay sleepily against Kane's shoulder. "I think you did the trick," she said quietly, feeling warm and soft inside as she looked at the two of them. It was another part of Kane she was discovering, and she liked it. She liked looking at the tenderness in his eyes, the soft smile as he talked to the baby.

After a few moments Kane gently lowered the baby into bed, covering him with a small white blanket. "Have a nice long sleep," he whispered, "and don't worry about taxes."

He straightened and grinned at Jenny, put his arm around her shoulders and led her out the door, turning the light low. He guided her into his bedroom and closed the door behind them. Then he took her in his arms and sighed.

"I haven't kissed you for hours."

She laid her head against his shoulder. "Were you looking for me when we found the baby crying?"

"Yes. I was watching you talk and laugh with Roger and I had the sudden urge to ravish you right then and there. Then someone claimed my attention and next time I looked you'd disappeared." He bent his head and kissed her. His mouth was warm and hungry and she pushed herself away with an effort.

"Tacky, tacky," she said, "smooching in the bedroom when you have a house full of guests."

He sighed again. "You bring out the worst in me."

"Thanks a lot!"

He laughed and took her hand, opened the door and propelled her out of the room.

In the guest room all was quiet.

"Well done," she said, squeezing his hand.

"Yes." His tone held a touch of sadness and she felt her heart contract. She knew he was thinking of Kevin. So much of his past belonged to other people—a woman she had never met, a child she had never known. Would she be able to make him happy again?

She was enjoying the party. She moved around the apartment, talking and laughing as they collectively ate their way through the plates of fancy hors d'oeuvres the caterers had delivered. Ordinary people. In many ways, they cer-

tainly were. They stood out by their lack of pretense.
Everybody was easygoing and the atmosphere was friendly
and relaxed. The circles her parents moved in were so very
different. There was always so much ego floating around it
was a pity you couldn't package it and sell it. Everybody was
out to impress everybody else. Here nobody was out to impress anybody.

It wasn't at all what she had expected. There was no
empty glamour, no pretense. The party showed her something altogether different.

Kane's friends were an interesting assortment of individuals and they all had one thing in common: they had made
something of themselves. They were creative, innovative
people and had battled all sorts of odds to make successes
of themselves. It was obvious what kind of people Kane
chose for his friends.

As the evening progressed, her enjoyment faded and she
became more and more depressed. She didn't fit in. Oh, she
got along well enough and she was having a good time, but
the fact was that she didn't belong.

Kane appeared out of nowhere. "Are you all right? You
look glum."

She forced a smile. "I'm fine. I guess it's late and I'm
getting tired."

"Kane?" It was Shana, smiling apologetically. "Sorry to
interrupt, but could I please use your phone?"

"Sure, right here." He opened the door to his study and
Shana went inside. He closed the door behind her and
looked back at Jenny.

"How about another drink?"

"Thanks. Some colombard, please."

"Don't leave, I'll be right back."

She leaned against the wall, surveying the room. She was
just beginning to wonder where Kane was with her wine

when his study door opened and Shana came out looking stricken.

"Where's Kane?" she asked, and her voice shook. In her hands was the photograph of Kane's wife and son, the glass shattered.

"He's . . . he's getting me a drink." Jenny stared at the picture. "I'll go find him." But before she could move, Kane was back, his eyes on the photograph in Shana's hand.

"Oh, Kane, I'm so sorry," she said miserably. "I knocked it off your desk by accident."

Putting the glass of wine on a side table, he took the picture from her hands and looked up. "It's only the glass, Shana. Don't worry about it."

"I'll have it replaced."

He shook his head. "I'll take care of it. And don't look as if you committed a crime. Go have a drink."

"There's glass on the floor." She gestured helplessly behind her and Jenny saw the glittering shards on the rug as they caught the light from the desk lamp.

"I'll get it." Jenny scooted away before Kane could say anything. She found a dustpan and a hand broom in a utility closet in the laundry room and carried them back into the study.

Kane stood at his desk, taking apart the frame and removing the remaining pieces of glass.

Jenny went down on her haunches and carefully swept up the glass. The tinier slivers were hard to get; the vacuum cleaner would have to take care of that. She straightened up and saw Kane open one of the desk drawers and put the picture away. As he closed it again, his eyes caught hers.

"I should have done that before."

Her throat went dry. "Why?"

"Because of you. It doesn't seem fair for you to have to look at it."

She grew very still. "You don't have to put it away on my account. She was your wife. He was your son."

"But I love you now."

Her heart lurched at the words, spoken so calmly, so quietly. "Oh, Kane," she whispered. Tears rushed into her eyes.

He strode to the door and closed it firmly, shutting out the party, the noise and the people. He wrapped her in his arms. "What's wrong?"

"It's not going to work, you know. You and I," she said thickly. "We don't belong together."

"Like hell we don't!" he muttered fiercely.

She leaned her head back to look at him. "Oh, Kane, don't you see? I don't fit in! All these people out there...they're your friends and..."

"Don't you like them? I thought you were enjoying yourself!"

"I was...I am. I do like them. It's not that. It's...they're all the same sort of people, don't you see? They're all so ambitious and creative and accomplished, or trying to be. I don't fit in with that sort of people. And you're one of them. I'm not right for you."

"You're creative and accomplished, too. You're just about to accomplish quite a creative project."

But I'm not ambitious and you do care about that, she thought, though she couldn't find the strength to utter the words. It was the real key to the issue, but they would never agree on that.

She moved away from his arms, smoothing her hair, and they stood looking at each other while the silence stretched.

"Apart from anything else you feel," he said softly, "do you love me?"

"Yes," she said and her voice shook. "You know I do." She began to cry. She turned away and leaned against the wall, tears running down her face. She wanted to pound the wall, bang her head, cry her eyes out, but when she felt Kane's hands on her shoulders, she turned and threw herself into his arms.

"I don't understand you," he said quietly. "But if we love each other, we can work out the rest."

Work it out? She didn't see how.

She didn't even believe it.

Kane couldn't help watching Jenny as she moved around the room talking and laughing with the guests. She looked sexy and sophisticated in the understated little silk dress, moving with a natural grace, comfortable with herself. Clearly, she was no stranger to this sort of affair; she was perfectly at ease.

Why then all those insecurities? He didn't understand what was going on in her head.

It would be very interesting to meet her parents.

The two men shook hands, sizing each other up.

Kane was as tall as her father, Jenny noticed. He was dressed in a light suit and tie and looked calm and confident as he greeted her parents. Most people, Jenny knew, tended to be intimidated by her father, by his sheer size and penetrating gray eyes. Not so Kane.

As they entered the sitting room, she wondered what Kane would do if her father treated him with the same thinly veiled contempt with which he treated David. He did not approve of David, a fact of which both David and Suzanne seemed oblivious. To Suzanne, David was the perfect man.

But Kane was not David, and her father recognized it instantly. Before long they were engaged in an animated discussion, and Jenny left them to help her mother in the kitchen.

"How old is he, Jenny?" her mother asked.

"Thirty-six. Ten years older than I am," she added unnecessarily.

"Is he divorced?"

"No. Widowed."

"Any children?"

She hesitated. "No."

Her mother carefully arranged slices of smoked fish pâté on small plates. "Isn't he a little old for you?"

"When I'm eighty, he'll be ninety. We'll both be dead or senile and it won't make a bit of difference."

"Are you planning to marry him?"

"Oh, I don't know," she said airily. "Maybe, maybe not."

"He seems a very sophisticated man."

"And all I do is grow cabbage." She sighed regretfully. "I know. It's hard to believe, isn't it?"

Her mother looked at her thoughtfully. She opened her mouth, ready to say something, then apparently changed her mind and pursed her lips. Fine lines radiated from her mouth. Her mother was getting older and it was showing, no matter how hard she fought it. No amount of creams and facials and massages would keep age from showing eventually.

There was silence as they put the finishing touches to the meal.

Jenny picked up the tray with the plates of pâté. "I'll take this in." She went into the dining room to distribute the plates. She heard her father's laughter coming from the living room. Making her father laugh was no mean feat. Clearly, Kane had already moved into her father's good graces.

The food was delicious. Perfectly broiled steak followed the pâté. Across the table Kane smiled at Jenny, a private little smile that gave her a thrill of delight.

"You have quite a talented daughter, Mr. McCarthy."

Jenny's father looked up from his steak, eyebrows raised. "Is that so?" His voice was carefully bland, not giving away any emotion.

"Have you seen what she has done with the wilderness around my house?" Kane asked, glancing over at her mother to include her in the question.

Her father shook his head. "No." He gave Jenny a quick glance from under his heavy brows. "She had not asked us to and I wouldn't think of trespassing on someone else's property."

And I haven't invited him, Jenny thought, spearing a piece of tomato with her fork. They had never told her they wanted to see it. And she wasn't going to beg for their approval or praise. Not ever again. She'd done too much of that when she was younger, wanting so much for them to value her accomplishments, too.

"I was going to wait until it was all finished," she said lightly, trying not to sound defensive. "And it almost is now. Except for the fall plantings, of course. They have to wait."

Kane looked around the table and gave one of his most charming smiles. "Maybe you and your wife would like to drive out one Saturday and have a look. Afterward I'd like you to be my guests for lunch or dinner—whatever works best. Unfortunately I can't entertain in the house yet, since it's only partially furnished."

"We'd like that very much," her mother answered, reciprocating with an equally charming smile.

Jenny chewed fiercely on a piece of meat. Here they were, the four of them in her parents' elegant dining room, with the best white tablecloth and flowers and beautiful food, smiling like idiots at each other. And you, Mr. Powell, she thought, are making quite an impression.

So, she said to herself, is that not what you want? You aren't surprised, are you? After all, Kane is handsome, successful and has made his way in the world. That's the sort of person they like. And he's charming, to boot. Of course they like him.

She struggled silently through her steak, giving up when it was only half eaten.

"Don't you like it, Jenny?" Her mother looked at her quizzically.

"I like it fine, Mom. It's just too much meat for me. I'm not used to eating so much."

"You do look thin."

She gripped her fork hard. "I am not thin, Mom," she said patiently. "I'm not any thinner than Suzanne."

Her mother frowned. "Suzanne works very hard. I think she forgets to eat sometimes."

Heat spread all through her body and her heart began to race with sickening speed. Suzanne worked very hard. After all, Suzanne was a lawyer and everybody knew how hard lawyers worked. Certainly harder than anybody who grew cucumbers and landscaped gardens.

"Nobody works harder than Jennifer has these last few months," Kane said smoothly. "You will understand when you see what she has done."

"Of course," her father replied. He gave Kane a penetrating look. "Why did you engage Jenny instead of a landscaping company?"

Kane shrugged lightly. "I saw the other work she had done and liked it. As I said, she's very talented."

Her father nodded, but made no comment.

Jenny came to her feet. She couldn't stand sitting there any longer. "I'll get the dessert," she said, taking her own plate and Kane's. Her parents didn't believe in her; they never had. All they knew was their disappointment in her—they saw or recognized nothing beyond that. Well, she didn't care anymore.

The doorbell rang. Suzanne and David. They'd been unable to come to dinner, much to Jenny's relief. They'd promised to come by later.

When Jenny came back into the dining room with the brandied peaches and cream, they were all engaged in a lively conversation. Suzanne was at her best. Give her a handsome, dynamic male to play up to and she positively blooms, Jenny thought nastily. Whatever she saw in David would forever be a mystery.

David was in great form. He bragged about his latest coup in real estate, speaking in sentences so convoluted with jargon it took an effort to make sense out of what he was saying. He was trying to impress Kane, who sat back in his chair, relaxed, listening with apparent interest. His face was serious, but Jenny noticed a barely contained smile in his eyes.

"I see," Kane said at last. "What you're saying, in plain English, is that . . ."

David's eyes narrowed as he listened. He straightened his back and gave Kane a haughty look. "That's right, however, in actual fact . . ."

Jenny suppressed a smile, noticing her father's look of bored disgust as another flow of verbiage rushed from David's lips.

"You're very quiet," Kane commented, as they drove back to Guilford later that evening.

"I'm trying not to scream."

He took her hand and squeezed it. "I did notice a certain strain at the dinner table."

"I try to be above it all," she said loftily, "but sometimes it still gets me."

"Isn't it possible you're just a little over-sensitive?" he suggested carefully.

She gave a humorless laugh. "You can't know what it means to have lived with their disapproval all these years. It's not blatant or out in the open, or anything like that. It's in all those little things. Like not asking me if they could come and see the garden. Like this idea of Suzanne working so hard. Oh, it's all kinds of things like that." She sighed. "I suppose in the final analysis it's their problem, not mine."

There was silence for a while.

"What did you think of them?" she asked at last.

"Your parents? I liked them."

She gave a small smile. "I thought you would."

One eyebrow rose in surprise. "You sound disappointed."

She shrugged. "It isn't that. I guess I'd hoped you'd understand how I feel about them, but you can't." She looked at him. "What did you think of Suzanne?"

"She's very beautiful," he said blandly.

"Apart from that."

"She's quite taken with herself. A little humility wouldn't do her any harm."

Jenny laughed. "Suzanne? Humble? She has nothing to be humble about. What about David?"

His mouth quirked. "David is a pompous ass, to use plain English."

Jenny burst out laughing. "Good. I'm glad we agree on that."

* * *

The blackberries were delicious.

She closed her eyes and savored the taste one by one as they practically melted on her tongue. They had done very well this year.

She sighed. She should be working, yet she felt so happy, so content just sitting on her porch looking out over her "kingdom," as her grandfather had always called it. It was still early in the morning and the heat of the day had not yet arrived.

She loved the peace and quiet, although the silence was deceptive. It was only the absence of human noises—cars, sirens, talking, laughing. Nature was alive and throbbing with sounds. There was the general background cacophony of soft cheeping and buzzing of insects hidden in the trees and grass. Now and then a burst of joyful twittering of a group of small birds would fill the air—busy, frantic sounds going back and forth and up and down, like the excited conversation of children.

She resented the drone of a plane, high overhead, disturbing the illusion of paradise. She smiled at herself. It always came, sooner or later. A car, an angry dog, the telephone.

She opened her eyes as she heard the sound of a car rounding the corner, then sat up straight as she recognized her father's Buick. Dad? she thought. What was he doing here in the middle of the morning? It had been months since he'd last visited her in her house. She leaped to her feet and walked to the car.

The door opened and he swung himself out of the seat, still lean and agile. He was dressed in an impeccable dark three-piece suit, an imposing figure waiting for her.

"Hi, Dad. What are you doing here?"

"Hello, Jenny." His gray eyes looked into hers and she stared back at him, feeling a sudden apprehension. She didn't know what was in his eyes, but she knew he'd never looked at her quite like this.

"I want to talk to you, Jenny."

Chapter Nine

Sure." She bit her lip. "Is everything all right? Is Mom—"

"Your mother is fine. Let's go inside."

They went into the kitchen. "Can I make you some coffee?"

He shook his head. "No." He sat down on a chair and leaned his arms on the table.

She folded the paper that lay spread out on the table, and sat down facing him. "Aren't you supposed to be at the office?"

"I was." He closed his eyes briefly and ran his hand over his forehead. "You have a new roof."

"I do, yes. The old one was in bad shape."

"I understand you took out a bank loan to pay for it."

Her body tensed. "So I did. And who told you that?"

He waved his hand in dismissal. "It doesn't matter." The steely gray eyes bored into hers. "Why didn't you tell me you were in trouble?"

"In trouble? I'm not in trouble."

"A bank loan of five thousand dollars is trouble for you," he stated flatly.

She could feel her heart begin to race with fury. Her hands trembled. "Dad, this is none of your business!"

"You're my daughter, dammit!"

"I'm your daughter, yes, but that doesn't give you the right to meddle in my business!"

He scraped his chair back and came to his feet. He frowned down at her and suddenly he looked very tired and old. "Jenny," he said, "why didn't you come to me? If you needed money, why didn't you come to me?"

She shrugged. "I don't know."

"You don't know? You have to know! What is more logical than asking your father for help?"

"I'm sorry."

"I don't want an apology!" he thundered. "I want an explanation!"

She looked at him squarely. "All right, then. I didn't want to ask you for help."

He looked stunned. "Jenny, I'm your father!"

"Yes, you're my father," she said dully.

"Doesn't that mean something to you?"

"Yes, that does mean something to me. My father is the man who doesn't approve of me. The man who doesn't approve of the way I've turned out. The man who doesn't think I can take care of myself, make responsible decisions, be independent. Well, I can take care of myself. And I am independent. I simply didn't feel like coming home to Daddy and asking him for help."

He stared at her, then sank heavily back onto the chair. "I see," he said.

"Do you?"

"Maybe. Maybe not." He picked up a matchbox from the table and turned it around and around in his fingers. "Your mother is worried about you."

"I don't think worry is the word. I think it's her inability to make me conform to her standards that's bothering her. I don't eat the way she thinks I should. My kitchen is dirty. My hair is too long. It's all very unacceptable to her."

"Is that the way you see it?"

"Yes, Dad, that's the way I see it."

There was a moment of silence. "I went to the Cleever house this morning," he said then. "Before I came here. I was so angry and disturbed I had to find a way to calm down before I faced you. So I went to the house and walked around in that garden of yours."

She felt her pulse quicken. *What did you think?* she wanted to ask, but her mouth could not form the words.

He watched her for a moment and she had the uncomfortable feeling that he knew what was in her mind, that he knew she was too proud to ask him what he thought of the work she had done, that she didn't want to admit that after all these years his approval was still important to her.

"I think Kane was right," he said at last. "I have a very talented daughter."

She hadn't known it would feel like this—such utter joy that tears sprang to her eyes. She lowered her gaze to the table, embarrassed by the emotions sweeping through her.

"Thank you," she said huskily.

There was an awkward silence. Her father cleared his throat and met her eyes. "I'm a good lawyer, they say," he began slowly. "I know how to discover the truth hiding behind people's words and expressions, to ferret out the real meaning and motives of their actions. But maybe when it comes to my own life and the people I love, I'm blind and ignorant. Maybe you, my own daughter, are my biggest failure."

He paused for a moment and she saw the sadness in his eyes and her heart contracted. And then came the realization that her father, the big-time lawyer, was vulnerable and that she had managed to hurt him by not calling for his help.

"Oh, Dad," she whispered.

"On Sunday, Kane told me how highly he thinks of you and of your work. I had to see for myself. And he was right. You are doing something wonderful with that garden." He smiled ruefully. "Where have we failed you, Jenny? We've always wanted the best for you."

"You always wanted me to be another Suzanne. And I'm not like Suzanne. I never was."

"No," he said, "you're not." There was no criticism in his tone. It was merely a statement of fact. Then he frowned. "You were always so damned stubborn. You never wanted to listen to what your mother and I had to say. You always seemed intent on thwarting us."

Maybe this was the time. At least this was the time she had. "Dad, are you ready to listen to me? Really listen?"

Something flickered in the gray eyes. "If you're ready to talk, I'm ready to listen."

It was not easy. She had to struggle for the right words, struggle to keep her emotions under control. But she let it all out, told him about all the times she'd been hurt and disappointed, about the pain of feeling like a failure, about resenting Suzanne for always being better at everything.

When she finished talking she took a deep breath and looked at him.

"You're wrong about one thing," he said. "I don't think, and I never did, that Suzanne is such a paragon." He smiled crookedly. "For one thing, a little humility wouldn't do her any harm. One day she's going to get her hands slapped."

Jenny gaped at him, then laughed. "That's exactly what Kane said, the humility bit."

"Kane is a smart man."

Sometimes, anyway, she amended silently. She got up from the table. "Can I make you some coffee now?"

He looked at his watch, then hesitated. "Please, but let me make a phone call."

As she made the coffee, she heard him talk to his secretary, telling her to cancel an appointment and postpone a meeting until later in the afternoon. *For me,* she thought, and her throat constricted. *He dropped everything this morning to see me because he was angry and upset that I hadn't come to him for help.*

When he was ready to leave some time later he took her hand a little awkwardly and gave a crooked smile. "I've never been very up front with my emotions, Jenny, but I want you to know that I love you and that I always have." He did not look like an imposing lawyer now and she felt an unaccustomed tenderness for him, a tenderness that closed her throat and blurred her vision. He looked into her eyes, and there was no stern coldness there. "And I'm sorry for not having been the father I should have been. All I really want is for you to be happy, and if this—" he made a sweeping gesture encompassing the house, the nursery— "if this makes you happy, then it's fine by me."

The tears came then, and she wiped them away hastily, trying hard to control them. She put her arms around him. "Oh, Dad," she whispered. "I love you, too."

She watched his car drive away, her eyes still misty. She felt a relief she could barely contain.

She stood at the window for a long time, thinking. Until the little blue and white van of the mailman caught her eyes and pulled her out of her absorption. She opened the door and walked out to the mailbox to meet him.

"Hi, Sam, how are you?"

"Okay, I guess. Arthritis is acting up a bit, but otherwise..." He handed her a bundle of mail and grinned. "Could be worse, you know. Lots of people are worse off than me. Emma-Jean can't hardly walk no more. Well, have a nice day, Jenny. Oh, yeah, my wife says to tell you the roses done real good this year.''

Jenny smiled. ''I'm glad to hear that.'' She gave a wave of her hand as he headed to the next mailbox down the road. She went inside, glancing through the envelopes in her hand.

Nothing interesting at first glance. A phone bill, several advertising leaflets—one telling her she couldn't live without a new fur coat, the other asserting she had no excuse not to buy a new sleeper-sofa. She tossed them into the garbage without a further look, then picked up the large manila envelope and ripped it open, frowning. It was sent by Kane's office in New York and she wondered what it could possibly be.

Uncomprehending she stared at the booklets and papers sliding out of the envelope. They had nothing to do with Kane's business. There was a course catalog from the College of Environmental Science and Forestry, State University of New York, Syracuse. There were application forms and other informational material.

All her joy and happiness seeped away. She stared at the papers, numb with anger and despair and a terrible sense of hopelessness.

She should have known all along. Kane would never give up. He was determined she would do what he wanted her to do. He could not accept her lack of ambition. He said he loved her, but it wasn't unconditional love.

What had ever attracted her to a man such as Kane? He wasn't for her. She wasn't for him. A dull despair settled in her heart.

In the long run they could never make each other happy.

''What hurts me the most is that you can't accept me the way I am! That somehow I don't measure up!'' Jenny took a deep, unsteady breath. Her knees were shaking, her hands clenched into fists by her sides. For the past few days, while she waited for Kane to come back to Guilford, her feelings had been fermenting with frightening speed.

"Why can't you accept me the way I am? Why can't it be enough?"

Kane came toward her and she stepped back. "Don't touch me!" She didn't know it was possible to look at someone you loved and feel such anger and pain. Her body was trembling with the force of it, her throat ached and the pain in her chest made it hard to breathe.

He didn't pay any attention, gripping her shoulders hard, looking into her eyes. "Listen to me, Jennifer!"

"And not even my name is good enough for you!" she said coldly. "Not grown-up enough, not sophisticated enough! Well, I've had it! How dare you send me that college catalog?"

"I didn't. I had intended to give it to you some time ago, but I changed my mind. My secretary must have found it on my desk and put it in the mail. I'd written your name on it."

"And how did you get it in the first place? You sent away for it, didn't you? The audacity! Don't you know what you're doing to me? You're trespassing on my self-esteem, on my self-respect! You have no right to move in on me the way you have—trying to change me, trying to make me into something I'm not!"

She felt her anger growing, pouring out of her every cell, and it felt like a poison, burning, hurting. She was shaking with it and she closed her eyes.

"You're wrong, Jennifer," he said calmly, and his quiet manner fired her fury.

"I'm not wrong! Don't you think I understand? I'm not stupid!"

"I don't want you to be anything you're not. What I want is for you to realize your potential, to develop your talent."

"Just like your clients! All those poor suckers tucked away in dark corners of the globe carving and weaving and painting and Lord knows what else! Well, I'm not one of them! I'm my own person with my own mind and I know what I want! So stay out of it!"

She tried to wrench herself free, but to no avail. His hands were like vices on her shoulders. She glared at him in impotent rage. He was pale under his tan and his jaws were clamped hard together. Good, she thought, he's having trouble controlling himself. Let him be mad, let him be good and mad!

"You're afraid to fail," he said softly. "You're scared of your sister and your parents, afraid of what they might say if you tried again and afraid of once more not making the grade."

She was stunned. "You're out of your mind!"

"They killed all your incentive and ambition," he went on, unperturbed. "Whatever you do is never good enough, so it's easier just to give up altogether. That way there'll be no more challenges and no more disappointments."

"So now you're an analyst, too," she said caustically. "You know everything, don't you? You understand it all."

"No, I don't. I'm only just beginning to work it out."

"Well, you have a long way to go before you've figured me out!"

His mouth twitched. "Probably."

She wondered what it would take to make him lose his cool. It was hard to keep her anger going when he wasn't giving her any fuel and she could feel it dissipate only to be replaced by a hollow despair. How could she fight him when he wasn't even listening to her? When he refused to understand? All he saw was his own hopeful image of her as a talented, ambitious professional.

"You're hurting my shoulders."

He slid his hands down her arms, but she moved away from him, looking at him coldly. She saw the pain in his eyes and her stomach cramped. He raked his hand through his hair and sighed.

"I'm sorry about the catalog. I had promised not to talk about you going back to school again, and I didn't intend to. I didn't send the catalog. Please, believe me."

"I believe you," she said tonelessly.

"I love you, Jennifer."

She felt her defenses crumble. Tears flooded her eyes. "Oh, God," she choked, "don't do this to me! Don't do this to me!"

"Do *what* to you?"

"Make me feel this way!" He said he loved her. She wanted to believe it, she wanted to believe it more than anything else. But he didn't love her; he only loved that fanciful idea he had of her.

"I don't understand," he said, shaking his head. "I told you I love you."

"Why?" Her voice was thick. "Tell me why."

"I could give you a thousand reasons, but they still wouldn't explain it. Chemistry, they say. Love is undefinable, intangible—like beauty and happiness. It's different for everybody."

"Then what do you like about me?" She had to have some answers, some sort of explanation. Something to hold on to.

He laughed. "Oh, Jennifer! You excite me, you intrigue me, you make me feel good, you're talented and enthusiastic and intelligent and stubborn and oh, well, I could go on." He smiled. "You make me happy, Jennifer McCarthy," he said softly. "You make me happy."

And it was there in his eyes and in his voice and she wanted to believe the truth of what he said. He reached out for her and this time she did not move away. He kissed her gently and she put her arms around him and closed her eyes. She didn't want to think anymore. She just wanted to hold him and love him. Love always seemed to win over her anger and fear. Maybe that was the way it was supposed to be.

He lifted his head. "There's something I want to talk to you about."

She caught something in his voice, and she drew back a little to look at his face. "What about?"

"This trip I'm taking next week will be my last for a while. Then I'll move into the house. There's no need for me to be in New York so much. I'll set up an office here and fly to New York from Syracuse once or twice a week. I think I'll like it better."

"You'll have lots of time to enjoy your garden."

"Yes." He smiled. "And while I'm gone on this trip, I want you to think about us getting married."

She grew very still and for a moment she forgot to breathe, then she expelled the air caught in her lungs. "Oh, Kane, I want to, only I'm not sure..."

"I know you're not. That's why I want you to think about it. I want you to move into the house with me, make it a home for both of us. I want to make you happy."

"I'm scared," she whispered.

He smiled. "You're supposed to be scared. Marriage is a big commitment."

"It's not marriage itself I'm worried about." She swallowed hard. "I love you Kane, but... but I keep thinking we're too different...."

He grinned crookedly. "That makes it interesting. And I want to make something clear before you give me an answer. I'm aware that you have qualms about the social aspects of my lifestyle. I know you don't like hopping from party to reception to dinner with people you don't know or care about. Sometimes it is important and necessary for me to attend these functions in New York or Boston or wherever. But as my wife you are not chained to me. I will not expect you to go to these with me if you don't want to. You are your own person and not an appendage to me."

"Thank you." He had considered her needs and her feelings in this, and warmth flooded her. She loved this caring side of him, the sensitivity, the gentleness. Yet there were other aspects of their relationship that worried her; his desire for her to be ambitious, to have a career.

The phone began to ring. With a sigh, Jenny moved away to pick up the receiver.

"Hello?"

"It's me, Mary. I wanted to let you know. It was so good, the best I ever had!" She was practically shouting into the phone and Jenny grimaced and held the receiver away from her ear. She glanced over at Kane who stood against the counter watching her.

"What was the best you ever had?" she asked.

"The tomato! My first one. It was as big as a basketball—well, almost, and so sweet and juicy, you have no idea!"

Jenny laughed. "Maybe I do, Mary, maybe I do."

"She sounded rather excited," Kane commented dryly after Jenny had replaced the receiver. "What was the best she ever had?"

"Her own very first home-grown tomato. As big as a basketball—well, almost."

He laughed, taking her hand. "Let's go over to the Garden of Eden and have a stroll. I want to see what wonders you have wrought this week."

Kane sat on the hotel terrace overlooking the Indian Ocean, wondering if he'd made a mistake. The sea glittered a crystal blue green and he narrowed his eyes against the glare. Overhead tall coconut palms rustled in the breeze and from the white minaret in the small town the muezzin began his chanting.

Such an idyllic place. A place made for romance. Yet right now he'd rather be in Jenny's kitchen drinking instant coffee and eating Oreo cookies.

A tall African woman walked barefoot along the water's edge, a baby on her back and a large basket of pineapples on her head. She moved gracefully, effortlessly, her arms swinging loosely by her side.

He wished for the thousandth time that Jennifer was with him, sitting across the table from him with that shine of excitement in her eyes. He would take her to explore the small town with it's whitewashed buildings, its mosques and its exotic blend of Arab and African culture. He would show her the fields of spiky sisal plants, the strange, exciting baobab trees, the wildlife.

Would she marry him? He wasn't at all sure. The memory of their last argument was still fresh in his mind. Why couldn't he get through to her? Every time he tried, it was like running into a wall. She didn't want to hear him. She didn't want to understand. He sighed, taking a swallow of his vodka.

What hurts me the most is that you can't accept me the way I am. He'd seen the pain shine through the anger in her eyes. He wondered if he had convinced her of his love—he wasn't at all sure of that, either.

Suddenly he felt afraid.

Around him were the voices of other people, the laughter of a small child. He glanced around. A young French couple sat not far away from him, talking with their little son who sat on the ground next to their table, playing with some toys.

Dark curly hair, dark eyes. Like Kevin.

He could never look at small boys and not think of Kevin.

* * *

Marrying Kane.

The thought was with her all the time. Jenny thought of nothing else as she put the finishing touches to Kane's garden, as she ate her solitary dinners, as she took care of the vegetables in her garden. In the middle of the night she awoke, worrying about it. In a way there was nothing she wanted more. She loved Kane. Being with him would be heaven, wouldn't it? She would live in his beautiful house. The garden she had designed with so much love would be her own. Maybe she could go on trips with him. They'd have children. Kane loved children. A happy life with the man she loved, and who loved her. How could she possibly not want it?

Yet she couldn't combat the fear that crept into her mind every time she thought of it. *He loves me now, but how long will it last?* Will he keep badgering me to do something with my "talent" as he calls it? Will he find a way to force me to go to school?

The thought was unbearable. She did not want to be coerced into anything.

Would he learn to love her the way she was? Would he eventually be able to accept that she wasn't ambitious?

Was it a risk worth taking?

One day she suddenly realized that the bulk of the work in Kane's garden was done. There was nothing to do but wait for the fall to plant the bulbs for spring flowers and the junipers and other evergreens.

Without the work on Kane's garden, the days stretched endlessly. She felt empty and depressed. The exhilaration she had felt earlier had faded and the high had worn off. She kept going back to the garden, strolling around, looking for something to do, something she might have forgotten or overlooked. There was nothing. Everything was done. Everything was just as she had always wanted it to be. It would grow more beautiful every year as the plants and shrubs became established.

She'd been so proud of the work she had done, of the big ambitious project she'd planned and executed so well, yet she seemed incapable of retaining the feeling. It was over and done with.

And I may never do anything like this again, she thought, denying it immediately. If Kane had given her this job, so might others.

But it might take years, her inner voice said. Well, there was plenty of other work. Like canning and freezing vegetables. Like washing the kitchen floor. Soon it would be time to sell mums and pumpkins.

She didn't want to sell mums and pumpkins.

She cried all the time and for the most ridiculous reasons or no reason at all. She cried in the bathroom as she was taking a shower. When she stubbed her toe, which didn't really hurt at all. When she spilled a glass of milk all over her clean kitchen floor. She cried as she picked peppers and tomatoes. She cried over coffee at Mary's.

"You know what it seems like to me?" Mary asked as she handed Jenny a box of tissue.

"I'd like to know." She wiped her eyes and blew her nose. "Oh, God, I've never felt so depressed in my life. I'm a constant waterfall. I don't even know why."

"I felt just like this, right after the baby was born. Baby blues. It's awful. You feel so helpless because you can't seem to control yourself and you're supposed to be happy, having the baby and not feeling like a buffalo anymore. I cried my heart out for weeks and weeks and almost drove Tom out of the house. He didn't know what to do with me."

Jenny nodded. "I remember. But I didn't have a baby, so I can't very well have the baby blues, can I?"

"No. Maybe you've got the garden blues."

"The garden blues?" She gave a short laugh. "Oh, Mary, come on now."

Mary poured them each another cup of coffee. "I'm serious. You put your heart and soul into that job. For months you've done nothing but think and plan and plant. I've never seen you so excited, so high on anything. And now it's done and there's nothing left. You're showing withdrawal symptoms, if you will. No wonder you feel depressed."

Jenny stared at her cup, frowning. "You think so?"

"I'm sure of it. What you need is another fix. Another job."

"Yeah, sure. Just like that. Guilford is full of Cleever houses with big gardens, and the owners are all standing in line to beg me to do them over for them."

Mary said nothing. She sipped her coffee thoughtfully, then carefully put down the cup. "Maybe you should go back to college," she said slowly.

Jenny stared at her speechlessly. "You've got to be kidding. Not you, too! I thought you were on my side!"

"I am."

"It doesn't sound like it to me! Don't you remember what you said before? I shouldn't let anybody push me into doing something I don't want to do!"

Mary sighed. "I know I said that. And I still think so. But I'm beginning to think you're your own worst enemy. That garden is magnificent, Jenny. But you may never again have a chance like it. Can you live with that? Can you honestly say you'll still be happy just growing flowers and vegetables and doing somebody's backyard now and then? There won't be much of a challenge to look forward to. Is that what you want?"

Jenny covered her face with her hands. "I don't know anymore," she moaned.

She didn't know anything anymore. The streets simmered in the morning heat as she drove home in the hot car, past the supermarket and the dry cleaner's and Billy James's hardware store.

Jenny wiped the perspiration from her forehead and sighed. When were they going to get a reprieve from this miserable heat? The grass was brown, the flowers were drying up. One of the workmen was coming in every day to water Kane's plants to make sure they didn't die. He'll have a surprise coming when he sees his next water bill, she thought. I'd better warn him.

He'd be back in another week. And he'd want her answer then.

She didn't know if she looked forward to or dreaded his homecoming.

The inevitable happened the next day.

The pickup truck refused to move. The engine engaged, but as soon as Jenny stepped on the gas and took her foot off the clutch, it died. Fear dried out her throat and she broke into a cold sweat. "Move, you decrepit old monster!" she muttered under her breath, turning the key once more. The engine sprang into life. She gave it gas, slowly let out the clutch and with a shudder the engine died. Four, five times she tried, every time with the same result.

She leaned her head on the steering wheel in utter defeat. It can't be true, she thought. Not this, too. Bad luck always comes in threes. She should have known. First the fridge, then the roof and now the pickup. The vehicle was fifteen years old. It was a miracle the truck had run as long as it had. She had no idea what was wrong now, but they'd probably tell her to take it to the dump and get a new one.

Which was exactly what she was told later that afternoon by the owner of Guilford Automotive Repairs.

"I'm sorry, Jenny," Ken Truman said apologetically, "but I can't, in good conscience, tell you to let me fix it.

You'd be back next month with something else. The truck has had it.''

She took a deep breath. "I appreciate that. I knew it was getting old and I expected it to be all over.''

And it's all over for me, too, she added silently. She could not run a business without a truck.

She sat at her desk that night, analyzing her finances, searching for a way to make payments on a new truck. There was no way.

"As I see it,'' she muttered to herself, "I can starve. Which is not productive. I can marry Kane and all my miseries will be over. Financial ones, anyway. We won't talk about the others.''

Marry Kane.

So he could buy her a pickup truck? Girl, you are losing it.

She could sell the house and the land, pay off the bank loan, buy a sporty little Mazda and go on welfare. Or apply for a job at the ice cream store. Or still marry Kane.

Why am I so depressed? she asked herself. Look at all the options I have!

She closed her cash book and her bankbook and shoved them back in the drawer. Wrong drawer. She yanked the stuff out again and her eyes caught the bright blue of the college application handbook.

There was one more option.

She could sell the house and the land, pay off the loan, buy a sporty red Mazda and go back to school.

She slammed the drawer shut, came to her feet, had a shower and went to bed.

She dreamed she was having dinner at her parents' house and told them of her plans. Her father was wearing a black judge's robe and a big curly wig. It seemed rather strange.

Her father wasn't a judge and judges didn't wear wigs, no
in the United States of America, anyway.

"I hope you know what you're doing," her father said
skeptically. "After all, it's been a while since you've been in
school. Are you sure you're not being too ambitious?" His
penetrating eyes scrutinized her over the rim of his reading
glasses. She suppressed a shiver and straightened her shoulders.

"Of course I'm being ambitious! Isn't that what you've
always wanted? Just watch me! I'm going to be the most
sought-after landscape architect in the state of New York
I'm going to have my very own company! I'm going to do
the grounds of big, beautiful mansions! You just wait and
see!" She felt a surge of exhilaration as she looked de
fiantly around the room at the faces of her parents and
Suzanne.

Her mother shook her head. "It won't be easy, Jenny
Science has never been your strong point. Or math."

"I used to have B's in math and science. B's are good! B's
are above average!"

"You're crazy," Suzanne said. "Landscape architec
ture? Why don't you do something that has a better fu
ture? Something in business or computers or health care."
She frowned. "Well, I suppose that might be a bit much for
you. The problem is, you've had your brain in mothballs for
so long, it might not function well anymore."

"And you have the sensitivity of a turnip! You may have
a brilliant mind, but it's nothing more than a computer! All
you know are rules and regulations and laws and statutes
All you know is how to read! You know nothing about
feelings and caring for others and your precious David is a
jerk!"

"David?" Suzanne asked. "Who's David?"

"I wish you'd cut your hair," her mother said. "And have you washed those windows yet? They were so dirty when I saw them last."

"I'm not going to cut my hair or wash my windows!" she screamed. "I'm not going into business or health care or computers! I want to work outside! I want to work with flowers and trees and plants and beautiful things! I'm going into landscape architecture and I don't care what you say or what you think or what you do! I don't care! You don't love me! You've never loved me for myself! I'm not ever going to do anything just to please you! I'm going to do what I want to do and I don't care if you like it or not! I don't care! I don't care!"

She struggled out of sleep, drenched with perspiration. Her feet were tangled in the sheets, her heart was racing as if she'd run a marathon.

"Good God," she muttered, staring dazedly at the ceiling. "I'm going nuts."

The sun streaked into the room and the jubilant chirping of birds wafted in on the breeze that puffed the curtains. She listened to the early morning sounds until her heart had calmed down and her breathing was normal again.

The dream played itself back in her mind. *I'm going to be the most sought-after landscape architect in the state of New York! I'm going to have my very own company!* She turned her face into the pillow and groaned. Where had all that come from?

She thought of the emptiness and the despair she'd felt ever since Kane's garden had been completed. *It's magnificent,* Mary had said. *But you may never again have a chance like it. Can you live with that?*

Can you live with that? Can you live with that?

She pulled the covers up over her face, as if she could block out the words. But there was no way to shut out the voices inside her.

You're afraid you'll fail.... It's easier just to give up all together. That way there'll be no more challenges and no more disappointments.

Maybe you've got the garden blues.... What you need is another job.... I'm beginning to think you're your own worst enemy.

Your own worst enemy. Your own worst enemy.

She jerked upright, picked up the pillow and threw it across the room with a smothered cry of frustration.

She climbed out of bed and marched barefoot into the kitchen to heat water for coffee. With the cup next to her on the desk for support, she opened the lower drawer and took out the catalog and the application handbook.

She wondered why they were in that drawer. Why had she never thrown them away? Good question, she commended herself. With a bit of creative thinking you might even come up with the answer.

Three cups of coffee and two hours later the forms were filled out and put into a manila envelope. She tore off several stamps from a roll and stuck them on the right-hand corner.

Her hands were trembling ridiculously as she began to write the address. Office of Admissions, State University of New York, College of...

Through the window she could see Sam's mail van slowly round the corner. She closed her eyes, feeling panic rise. She finished quickly and rushed out the door to meet him. Her legs felt like lead.

She handed Sam the envelope with a feeling of doom, her hand still trembling. She watched him drive away, forcing down the panic.

It's too late now, she thought. I've done it. I've actually done it.

Kane called early Thursday afternoon.

"I just got back. I'll change clothes and look through my mail and then I'm off. I'll see you this evening."

"I'm glad you're back."

"So am I." He paused. "Jennifer, we need to talk. There's something I have to tell you."

"What is it?" The serious tone of his voice frightened her.

"I'll tell you tonight. I don't want to talk about it over the phone."

Her knuckles were white as she gripped the receiver. *Too late!* she thought. *He changed his mind. He doesn't want to marry me anymore. He finally realized he's making a mistake.*

Her legs began to shake and she sat down on a kitchen chair, clutching the receiver to her ear.

"Jennifer? Are you still there?"

"Yes," she squeaked. She cleared her throat. "I'm still here."

"Are you all right?"

"I'm fine." She swallowed as she looked at the college catalog on the desk. "I have something to tell you, too."

There was a silence. "You want to tell me now?"

"No. It'll wait. We'll talk when you get here."

"All right, then." His voice sounded strange and there was a minute of silence. "Jennifer," he said at last, "I . . ." He hesitated. "Never mind. I'll see you later."

"'Bye, Kane."

She replaced the receiver, staring blindly at the wall. There was a sick feeling in her stomach, and she noticed her hands were clammy.

Something was wrong.

Chapter Ten

By the time the gray Continental pulled up in front of the house, Jenny was a mass of nerves. All afternoon she'd imagined what it could possibly be that he wanted to tell her. Something that was too important to discuss over the telephone. Of all the things that she could come up with, only the one that had first entered her mind made sense: he didn't want to marry her anymore. He'd finally realized that she wasn't the right person for him, that she couldn't possibly keep him happy for any length of time.

Well, I'll live, she thought bravely. *No, I won't. I'll die.* But nobody these days died of a broken heart. She wasn't the first one to have an unhappy love affair. No, two. Oh God. There were women who made a career of unhappy love affairs. Maybe she was one of them. No, she'd rather die. She could cook up some rhubarb leaves and... She was coming unhinged, no doubt about it.

She had everything to live for. After all, wasn't she on her way to becoming the most sought-after landscape architect n the state of New York? Maybe even in all of New England? She didn't need a man. If Kane didn't want her anymore, she could do without him.

Her stomach clenched into a hard ball as she watched Kane stride to the door. His tan was deeper than ever and he looked fit and lean. He was wearing lightweight slacks and a sky blue polo shirt. He raked his hand through his hair, which seemed rather on the long side. She liked the look of it.

She opened the door and for a moment he just stood there gazing at her with his eyes dark and serious and her heart began to drum in her ears.

"Hi," she managed.

"Hello, Jennifer."

They didn't move, but stood looking at each other in a sudden awkward silence, a silence that screamed in her ears. He didn't kiss her or embrace her and the fear grew into numb despair. She turned away and filled the kettle with water.

"Would you like some coffee?"

"Please." He pulled out a chair and sat down, raking his fingers through his hair again. She'd never seen him so uncertain before.

"I kept some dinner for you. I wasn't sure if you would stop for something."

"I didn't. But I'm not hungry. Thanks anyway."

Another silence.

"Did you have a good trip?" she asked in an effort to say something, anything.

He nodded absently. "Signed two contracts."

She took two mugs from the cabinet and spooned coffee into them. "The garden is finished. There's about a week's work left in the fall to plant the bulbs and the junipers and other evergreens. The rest is all done."

All done! All done! The words reverberated in her head
The garden was all done. Her relationship with Kane was al
done. Her business was all done.

"Thank you. I'll have a look tomorrow." He sounded lik
a polite stranger. God, she couldn't stand this for anothe
minute.

"Of course, next spring there'll be more to do. There's th
planting of the annuals and . . ." She was babbling, and sh
kept going until the kettle shrieked and made her stop.

She poured boiling water into the mugs. Carefully pick
ing them up, she moved over to the table and sat dow
across from Kane.

"So," he said, looking straight at her. "What was it yo
wanted to tell me? I don't imagine it was about the wonder
of petunias." He smiled faintly, but it didn't reach his eyes

"You said you had something to tell me."

"Ladies first."

"I've sent in my application to the State University o
New York."

Surprise flared in his eyes. He straightened his back an
stared at her for a speechless moment. Then he shook hi
head, as if in a daze. "No, Jennifer, no. I don't want you t
do that."

I don't want you to do that. I don't want you to do tha
The words echoed in her head. He didn't want her to go
Because it didn't matter anymore. Because he didn't wan
her anymore. She sat down on a chair, swallowing at he
panic.

"Why?" she whispered. "It's what you wanted me to d
ever since you've known me!" She tried hard to control th
quaver in her voice. "Is it because you don't want to marr
me anymore?" She braced herself for the answer.

She had not expected the baffled expression on his face
"Because I don't want to marry you? What are you talkin
about? Of course I want to marry you!" He pushed back hi

chair and came to his feet, walked around the table and pulled her up out of her chair. "Jennifer," he said huskily, "where in hell did you get that idea?"

She slumped against him. "I thought that's what you wanted to tell me. And then...then when you got here...you were so distant, you seemed so strange. You didn't even kiss me. I thought it had to be true. I'd thought about it all afternoon."

"And I thought all afternoon that you were going to tell me the same thing. That you had decided you didn't want to marry me."

She swallowed at the constriction in her throat, then gave a hysterical little laugh. "Oh, God, no. No... I was going to tell you about going back to school." She looked up at him and shook her head. "I don't understand. Why don't you want me to go anymore?"

He smiled crookedly. "That's what I wanted to tell you. I did a lot of thinking these last few weeks—about you and me, about the things you told me. I don't want you to get a degree for me. I forced you into it. It was wrong. I had no right to pressure you." He looked at her closely. "You told me I was trespassing, and you were right. I was arrogant to presume I know what's good for you and what isn't. I had no right to tell you what to do with your life. And I'm sorry, Jennifer, I'm sorrier than you'll ever know that I've made you so unhappy."

There was a lump in her throat and joy began to quiver through her. "You made me happy, too."

"Oh, Jennifer! I love you! I don't care if you get that degree or not. Please, please, don't go if you're doing it to make me happy. You don't need to do it for me; that's never what I intended. I love you just the way you are. Forget about school."

"But I've already sent in my application."

"You can withdraw it."

"Do you really mean that?"

"Yes. I was wrong, Jennifer. All I want is for you to be happy."

She sighed, then gave a small smile. "You're not going to believe this, but I don't want to withdraw it. I did some thinking, too. All this time I thought I was fighting you. Well, I was wrong; I was fighting myself, my own fear, my own cowardice. You were right about that, and I was too stupid to see it."

"What were you so frightened of?"

"Of failing, I guess. Just like you said. And of what my parents were going to say. They've always been so skeptical of my capabilities. They always seemed to think I couldn't do anything right."

But not anymore, she thought. *Dad knows. He understands me now.* And the joy of it was still there.

"Won't they be happy to see you go back to school?"

"I think they will be." She sighed. "But apart from everything else, I'm still scared. I know it sounds dumb, but I can't help it. But that's no way to go through life, is it?"

He smiled. "No, it isn't."

She bit her lip. "I know I've got to try. For myself. Dropping out of college, taking over the nursery... it was all an act of defiance, I know that now. I was so unhappy, so angry with my parents for putting me in a competitive situation with my sister that all I wanted was to get out of it. So, that's what I did. Subconsciously I must have figured that if I didn't try to make something of myself then I couldn't fail, either, could I? You were right about that, too. I took care of everything in one fell swoop." She grimaced. "Took away my own future in the process."

He gave her a long, assessing look. "What made you change your mind? Three weeks ago you were raving at me for not wanting to accept you for what you are. Why all the insight suddenly?"

"I finished work on the garden."

"So?"

She made a helpless gesture. "I was miserable. There was nothing else to do and suddenly I felt so useless, so empty. I was so depressed, I was beginning to worry about myself. I was crying all the time for nothing. And then it hit me. I didn't want to go through life and never do that again, never get another chance. I enjoyed it so much. It was such a wonderful job. And the thought that I might never do anything like it again scared me senseless. I've never been so miserable in my life." She chuckled. "You know what Mary called it? The garden blues."

"The *what*?"

She laughed at his puzzled expression. "My state of mind reminded her of the way she felt when she had the baby blues after Justin was born." She paused for a moment. "And then everything happened. The pickup broke down and I didn't know how I was going to go on and..." She took a deep breath and laughed again. Suddenly laughter came easily. Suddenly nothing seemed so awful as it had before. "One thing led to another. It seemed the only thing to do was sell everything, buy a little car and try my luck elsewhere."

"You don't need to sell if you'd rather keep the property, Jennifer. I know the place means a lot to you."

"But..."

"I don't want to hear it!" he threatened.

"Hear what?"

"About you not wanting to be financially dependent on your husband."

She frowned. "I have to admit I'm not crazy about the idea. It's going to cost thousands of dollars to—"

"Shut up," he said, and silenced her with a kiss. "It'll be a great investment, don't you realize that? I have an instinct for profitable business deals and this is one of them."

"Well, if you say so."

"I say so." He looked at her solemnly. "So, will you marry me?"

Warmth flooded her. "Yes, yes!"

"And you really, truly want to go back to school? Out of your own free will?"

"Yes," she said with conviction. "Out of my very own free will."

"And not because I wanted you to?"

"No. You were right about that, too, you know."

"About what? About you going back to school?"

"No. About being arrogant and presuming you knew what was or wasn't good for me." She smiled sweetly.

"Don't be nasty, sweetheart."

"Okay." She touched her mouth to his. A thought occurred to her and she withdrew slightly. "What about children?" she asked softly. "I know you're looking forward to being a father again. If I go back to—"

"Shh." His arms tightened around her. "First we'll get used to being married. It'll only take you two or three years to get your degree, anyway. We'll work it out. First things first." He kissed her nose. "I love you," he said. "Everything will be fine."

She let out a deep sigh. "I feel so much better, you've no idea. Now if I can just get over those anxiety attacks when I think of sitting in stuffy classrooms." She shuddered delicately and he laughed.

"You'll manage, I'm sure."

"I'm glad you've got so much confidence in me."

"I have a knack for discovering treasures, and you're my find of the year. Of course I have confidence in you."

"Find of the year! Gee, you make me feel so good!"

He laughed and hugged her to him. "Would you like me to call you Jenny?"

"No." The answer was instantaneous. "You were right about that, too. It's too childish. I feel more like a Jennifer now."

He grinned devilishly. "Just remember from now on: I'm always right."

Her outraged protest didn't have a chance. He held her tight, kissing her until she had no breath left for words.

*   *   *   *   *

Keepsake

 Harlequin Books

You're never too young to enjoy romance. Harlequin for you . . . and Keepsake, young-adult romances destined to win hearts, for your daughter.

Pick one up today and start your daughter on her journey into the wonderful world of romance.

Two new titles to choose from each month.

COMING NEXT MONTH

#634 HILLBILLY HEART—Stella Bagwell
Morgan Sinclair had been waiting for Lauren Magee to return to him for years—but he never expected his first love to come back with such a startling secret....

#635 MAYBE NEXT TIME—Joan Smith
When future congressman Patrick Barron demanded Elinor Waring return the love letters he'd written, he was up for the toughest part of his campaign!

#636 PRETTY AS A PICTURE—Patti Standard
Erika Lange was shocked to discover an indiscreet photo of herself in a magazine—but it all clicked when she met publisher Richard Marlow....

#637 WOMAN OF THE WEST—Nora Powers
Hope Crenshaw had disguised herself as a man to get a job as a rodeo clown. Pete Hamilton wasn't fooled—and found himself enjoying the charade!

#638 SOMEONE TO LOVE—Brenda Trent
When no-nonsense businessman Greg Bradford arrived at Lilly Neilson's bed-and-breakfast inn, she knew that getting the handsome workaholic to relax would take some extra effort....

#639 A TRUE MARRIAGE—Lucy Gordon
Gail Lawson had vowed to marry the first man she bumped into—and a mysterious stranger, Steve Redfern, was more than happy to block her path....

AVAILABLE THIS MONTH

#628 THE TENDER TYRANT
Victoria Glenn

#629 ALMOST AN ANGEL
Debbie Macomber

#630 RHAPSODY IN BLOOM
Mona van Wieren

#631 STRANGER AT THE WEDDING
Joan Mary Hart

#632 HEART TO HEART
Marie Ferrarella

#633 A MOST CONVENIENT MARRIAGE
Suzanne Carey